# LUKE'S REVENGE

*NEW YORK TIMES* BESTSELLING AUTHOR
## LISA RENEE JONES

ISBN-13: 979-8354246922

Copyright © 2022 Julie Patra Publishing/Lisa Renee Jones

All rights reserved. No part of this publication may be reproduced, distributed, or transmitted in any form or by any means, including photocopying, recording, or other electronic or mechanical methods, without the prior written permission of the publisher, except in the case of brief quotations embodied in critical reviews and certain other noncommercial uses permitted by copyright law.

To obtain permission to excerpt portions of the text, please contact the author at lisareneejones.com.

All characters in this book are fiction and figments of the author's imagination.

www.lisareneejones.com

# DEAR READERS,

It's finally time for the conclusion of Luke (or is it Lucifer?) and Ana's story. I always like to guide you back into the world when we start a new book, so here is a brief recap. Ana and Luke met when Luke was discharged from the military. Luke aka Lucifer, as a nickname, is a pilot but there is more to his trade and his story. What is that story?

Luke and Ana's stepfather, Kurt, cross paths for the first time while seeking the same hostile target and become united against an enemy they go on to defeat. This mission represents the killer Luke has become and while he doesn't like this part of his life, it's his duty, a duty that slowly eats away at him. Ultimately though, it's years later when he leaves the military, and only after yet another close friend is killed, which marks too many dead friends. As a civilian he opens a contract-for-hire business, running legit, high-paying, but often dangerous jobs overseas.

Luke meets Kurt's stepdaughter, Ana, who is an FBI agent, when he visits Kurt looking for men for a mission.  Kurt trains men to be assassins for the government. Kurt also raised Ana and her brother, Kasey, when their mother was murdered by one of Kurt's enemies. Ana and Kasey lost their father when they were young to a car accident.

The attraction between Ana and Luke is instant, and Luke isn't about to let Ana slip away. Not an easy task when Ana avoids men who have connections to Kurt, men training, or trained, to be government assassins. Luke, however, won't take no for an answer. He pursues her with intensity and determination, a man who has found what he wants and will not accept anyone else. Fortunately for him, Ana falls hard for him. From there, the perfect love story between them seemed to form.

Luke proposes to Ana and she accepts. After this commitment is created, Luke is driven to work harder, to do more for Ana in the future. He continues to work his high-risk jobs, at least, long enough to surprise Ana by buying her the horse ranch she'd always wanted, and more. Flash forward, Ana's stepfather, Kurt, is killed on a government assignment. The facts are few, and all of the circumstances surrounding his death felt off. Even Kurt's right-hand man, Jake, refuses to talk about the job, claiming it's top secret.

Oddly, to Luke, Kurt leaves his home, and training facility, The Ranch, to Kasey, not Ana, when Kasey was a bit of a fuckup, and incapable of taking over the operation. Additionally, Kurt, a wealthy man at the time of his death, leaves Kasey no money to fund The Ranch. Even odder, Ana's inheritance is sealed, not to be opened for years to come.

Another year passes and Luke has planned a couple of final, high-paying jobs, before he shut down his overseas operations. Meanwhile, Kasey is struggling to maintain The Ranch with no cash. As a favor to Ana, Luke took Kasey on one of his final big jobs.

It's on this mission in Egypt while transporting a princess to safety, that Kasey chooses to run a side job, and Luke intervenes. Everything turns south from there. Kasey kills several of Luke's men and then holds a gun to the head of the princess. A standoff ensues between Luke and Kasey and Luke can see in Kasey's eyes that he is about to shoot. Luke is forced to kill Kasey. He's devastated and Ana will be heartbroken.

It gets complicated from there, as if it's not complicated enough already.

When Luke goes home to tell confess all to Ana, one of the men on his team that was working with Kasey,

Trevor, has already found his way to her side. Ana knows about Kasey and Trevor has a painted a dirty picture in which Luke was the dirty one, and Kasey tried to intervene. Ana is freaked out, angry and crying. She ends up shooting Luke or so he thinks. Nothing was as it seems. Ana was actually trying to save him from Trevor when the shuffle made her gun slip from her hand. When she'd tried to catch it, the weapon had gone off.

Now, we're in a quandary.

Luke believes Ana shot him on purpose and in Ana's grief over her brother, she does a horrible job of clearing that up.

They break-up and Luke moves away, and soon after, is recruited by Walker Security.

During the two years that follow, the two of them are miserable and angry without each other, but destiny ensures they find each other again. On a training event with Walker, Luke receives a call from Jake, Ana's godfather, and Kurt's ex-right-hand man. Jake is frantic, warning Luke "they," whoever they are, plan to kill Ana. Jake is murdered while Luke is on the phone with him. The man on the phone challenges Luke to get to Ana before him. Luke is desperate to save Ana, the woman he still loves. He arrives to her location just before she is attacked. Despite her negative reaction to seeing him, the fire is there between them and soon Ana and Luke are on the run, in a tug of war of lust, love, anger, and even hate, while everyone around them could be an enemy.

Turns out, the day Kasey died, the package he was transporting disappeared. That package is important, and for reasons they don't understand, the people he was working for have suddenly decided Ana or Luke have that package. A hitlist of everyone who was present on the mission the day Kasey died is discovered as well. One of Luke's old employees, Parker, barely escapes a hit and joins Ana, Luke, and the Walker team to try to end this mess. Luke, with Walker Security's help, reaches out to everyone on the list, to warn them of the danger they are in. Ultimately, Ana learns that her ex-partner, Darius, was dirty and working for the bad guys, keeping an eye on her, and searching for the package.

When Ana meets up with Darius, he is killed in front of her, but not before he slips a phone into her jacket. The bad guys call that phone and demand the package. Luke negotiates to find it—for a price, and by a certain deadline.

Meanwhile, Ana discovers Darius left her more than a phone. He left her a clue which leads them to his cabin and a tape recorder with a message. Darius tells Ana, via the recording he's left her, that her boss, Mike, is dirty, as are many influential people in the city. He also references a key and a lockbox that Ana and Luke have yet to explore at the end of *Lucifer's Touch*. This locker is supposed to contain pictures and data that expose their enemies.

Ultimately, Kasey was working for a large organization that buys and sells priceless items that are often stolen. Darius has a list of buyers, including the one who was supposed to buy whatever Kasey was transporting. Darius seems to have known a lot of things, but what he didn't know, was the identity of the big boss behind all of this. Perhaps he was close to finding out when he died.

Ana and Luke attempt to question that person but find him dead. Later they also learn that Mike, her boss, has been killed in a car accident, and they are certain his death is a murder. Seems everyone that might lead them to whoever the big boss is, ends up dead.

Ana and Luke decide it is time to hole up at her father's old property, The Ranch, where they can take both a defensive and offensive position. They arrive there and nothing goes as planned. I'm going to share the last scene of *Luke's Touch* with you now to bring you back into the moment...

—*Lisa*

# FINAL SCENE OF BOOK ONE

## ANA

We bring The Ranch into view and I swear I feel it like a punch in the chest, the way I did right after Kurt died. Everything feels unsettling where Kurt comes into play. Everything I thought I knew; I no longer believe I know at all. Nothing is as it seems. Who knew just how real those words would become. Luke and I are not over, for starters. In fact, we're engaged again. That alone is one of the wonders of the world.

If only everything I thought I knew, but didn't know, translated to something as wonderful as finding Luke again.

But it doesn't, and outside of the Darius revelations, there are more coming. Soon. Really soon. I feel it in my bones.

Luke drives us through the gate openings to the property which is miles and miles of land, all of which is a mock battlefield, complete with hidden tunnels, booby traps, and mind games. Kurt was always so good at mind games. He played them with me from the time I was a young girl. I know first-hand that this is a place that makes boys into men and men into warriors and in some cases, monsters. They also made a little girl who loved Barbie dolls into an FBI agent.

The central property, which was Kurt's home, allows for public entry. A necessity considering the training operation this place housed.

"We won't have garage access," I tell him.

"I'll pull to the rear and after we ensure the house is clear, we'll pull into the garage out of sight."

I nod, that twisty feeling in my belly tightening a bit more. I hate being here today when this place should be empowering. I know it as I know my own name. Intimately, automatically, perfectly. Luke pulls us to the rear of the house, as the rental doesn't have a connection to the garage, with plans to hide our presence by moving the vehicle later.

Luke's phone rings and he answers with, "Where are you?" then glances in his rearview.

I turn to find another SUV headed our way. *The rest of our team*, I think.

"Pull to the rear," Luke informs them, confirming their identity.

Once we're parked, Luke and I head to the door. I unlock it and we step inside and my gut goes wild. I instantly know something is wrong. Or maybe this place just feels wrong to me now, because I don't know the man who once lived here. He had secrets. I'm not sure what to think about, just how deeply they seemed to run. Luke walks toward the kitchen to clear the property. I am drawn to Kurt's office, almost as if a magnetic field drags me in that direction. I step to the center of the double doors and my breath hitches.

Kurt is sitting at the desk.

He stands up, tall, and healthy looking, his body fit, his face full, but still chiseled. Almost as if he's been on a really good vacation.

"Ana," he says. "It's been too long." He rounds the desk and steps in front of me, and I can see the green of his eyes, with the little orange flecks that reminded the sixteen-year-old me of the fires of hell when he was screaming training commands at me.

I stand there, stunned, unable to move, my feet planted on the ground as if the carpet were cement. "How are you here? What is this?"

"What the fuck, Kurt?" Luke demands, stepping to my side.

I'm remotely aware of a door opening and of footsteps behind the three of us, and I want to shout for them to leave, to allow us time to process and claim the answers we deserve. That *I* deserve.

"Everything is not what it seems," Kurt says. "It's a lot worse, Ana."

"What does that mean?" I demand, my voice trembling, while Luke's possessive, protective energy pops beside me.

"Start talking, Kurt," Luke demands tightly, and it's really not a shock when he draws on him, aiming his weapon at him, "because I haven't decided if I should be celebrating right now or shooting you."

Suddenly the dynamic changes. Another person enters the picture. "Kurt, you bastard. You really need to just die already, but at least I can finally make you pay properly for your stupidity."

I whirl around to find Parker holding a gun over my head, pointing it at Kurt. Adam and Savage are not here, at least not at this moment, and I don't know why. I can barely process what is happening. Why is Parker here and they are not? I never get a chance to ask. The next thing I know I'm grabbed from behind and Kurt has a hold of me, with a gun pointed at my head.

He eyes Luke and issues a command. *"Kill him."*

I'm his shelter because he fears Luke will kill him. And I think he might have to.

My fiancé was forced to kill my brother. Now I think he might be forced to kill the only man I've ever really looked at as a father.

# CHAPTER ONE

## LUKE

The roar of blood rushes in my ear, while the lightning burn of adrenaline shoots through my veins, a familiar call to action. I have about three seconds to process what has happened and where that leads me, but I'm in a familiar place, in a zone where I'm outside myself and the room, assessing the scene below.

Me holding a gun pointed at Kurt. Him holding a gun to her head, his own *daughter*. Parker holding a gun pointed at Kurt and shouting at him like he knows him. Kurt shouting at me to kill Parker, which means turning my gun away from Kurt, and in turn, leaving Ana exposed.

That requires me trusting Kurt not to kill Ana.

Kurt, who pretended to be dead, and was not.

That's a fucked up reality that I don't have time to fully get my head around right now. What matters now is that he's forcing my hand, making me choose to kill him or Parker, and gambling that I know him well enough to know he did what he did for a good reason.

He's not wrong.

But I'm also not stupid. Kurt's motivation to push me to kill Parker reads like his desire to shut Parker up before he talks too much. And the fact that I believe this to be the case, means I don't trust Kurt at all. Decision made.

I slide my arm left, shoot the gun out of Parker's hand, and then for good measure, pop another bullet into his thigh. Before Parker ever hits the ground, my weapon is retrained on Kurt. Parker begins to howl in pain, and I kick his gun away, watching Kurt, who's still holding Ana. Making damn sure Kurt knows that he's next if he doesn't do what I expect and drop his weapon.

He has three seconds and I don't warn him of that fact.

He knows how this plays out. He created the three-second rule.

One.

Two.

He releases Ana, his gun lowering to his side, but he doesn't drop it. His eyes meet mine, a pulse, a tension, and a challenge, between us. But this man knows me, and more than my skills, my willingness to kill. Therefore, my finger on the trigger, ready to squeeze, is the only answer to that challenge he needs.

"I kept him alive to hear what he has to say," I say. "Give me a reason to keep you alive real damn fast."

Ana steps up to him, points her gun at his head, and says, "Drop the weapon," her voice a low, tight band, threatening to break.

Only Kurt doesn't comply. Abruptly and suddenly, instead of dropping his weapon, he aims beyond me, toward Parker or maybe beyond, and at the door. Which I can't know unless I turn and I have no choice but to do just that. I step sideways, just enough to ensure we aren't being attacked, and it's already too late to save Parker. Kurt plants a bullet in his head. Parker is dead. Kurt sets his weapon on the ground and lifts his hands. "He was about to shoot you, son."

I don't immediately accept or reject that explanation.

I assess the potential danger. Ana's gun remains pointed at Kurt. The doorway is clear. With those things confirmed, I eye the weapon lying next to

Parker's left hand. I don't know if he's ambidextrous, because apparently, I didn't know shit about Parker, besides yes, he had another gun. That's clear. What's not clear is who he intended to shoot. My weapon swings back to Kurt.

"I'm unarmed," Kurt declares. "If I was trying to do you dirty, I wouldn't be. You know that about me."

I'm as certain of that as I am the next lotto pick numbers. I don't really know that he's unarmed. Parker damn sure wasn't. And as for his "son" address, twice now, "It's Lucifer to you," I say, "and we both know how Lucifer feels about killing. I'll drop you like a rock and live with the consequences of Ana's pain later. Don't play me, man. You wanted to shut him up."

His eyes light with smug amusement. "And yet we both know you're carved inside out just thinking about killing me. Because you know it'll kill her."

I don't argue his statement as right or wrong. I just look at him. I don't even remind him I killed Kasey. Sometimes what's in the eyes is what speaks a thousand words.

His eyes narrow on my face, a tic in his jaw before he clearly sizes me up as willing to shoot because he defends his actions when Kurt never defends his actions. "I didn't *need to* shut him up. I came here to tell you both everything."

"You could have told us everything before we went to your funeral," Ana snaps. "And you're not talking. You're not saying anything besides 'please kill me' that I can hear right now. Because every single time you open your mouth that's what I hear."

He turns to face her, but considering her gun is aimed right at him, not a tremor to her experienced grip, he smartly keeps his own hands in the air. Kurt is reaping the rewards of his own parenting, facing off with an emotionless daughter he created with his constant drills. He did the same to Kasey, only Kasey didn't know how to be a warrior *and* a man. It was one or the other, and in the end, he lost his humanity. But knowing Kurt as I do, Ana's weakness in his mind is that she never did, which is exactly why he softens his voice and says, "Ana, baby girl."

I also know Ana.

He's miscalculated his approach and his little "baby girl" endearment is not the right thing to say.

Her jaw clenches, her anger spiking in the air, her desire to punish him, a living, breathing creature in the room. All that saves him is Ana's experience, maturity, and probably her badge. While there are obviously too many that do not, she cares about her duty, and it checks her actions. In truth, it checks the extreme actions Kurt taught us all that could easily have defined Ana in the wrong ways.

As it did Kasey.

With her badge as a part of her core makeup, she steps outside the moment, saving her meltdown for later, and if I have my way, in my arms, when we're alone. Unless I kill Kurt. Then I don't know what happens, but ultimately it can't matter. I can't let it change what happens next because bottom line, I won't allow her to be put in a position to kill Kurt. If he has to die, it has to be me who pulls the trigger, not her.

And I know Kurt.

At any moment, he could make a move that forces her hand.

For that reason, I move toward Ana, intending to place myself in between him and her, when the front door opens. Before I can even turn, I hear Savage murmur, "Mother of God." I bring him and Adam into view as they both pull their weapons. "Who the hell do I need to kill?" Savage asks. "I'll ask why later."

"I think Ana has that under control," Adam replies. "The man she's presently holding a gun on is Kurt, her stepfather, whose funeral I believe she went to, roughly three years ago."

Information me and a bottle of tequila gave him about a year ago somewhere in Iraq.

"Someone please come tie him up before I shoot him and make him dead for real, possibly enjoying it way too much for me to wear my badge. And I like my badge."

Adam casts me a lazy, cool-as-a-cucumber look because he is cool as a cucumber and asks, "Any idea where I can find rope?" No wonder I like him. He's a fucking badass.

"Garage," Ana supplies. "Far left wall, in the storage bin." Her eyes remain fixated on Kurt, a blistering anger in their depths. "You claim you came here to tell us everything. Try opening your mouth and speaking words."

"Everything I did was to protect you, Ana."

Ana gives a choked laugh that still manages to remind me of a princess at a ball, elated as a new song begins to play and inviting everyone to join in a playful dance number. Her delicate delivery of even the worst subject matter is part of what makes her a deadly package. The enemy never sees her coming, even when she's standing in front of them.

"There's that word again," she says. "*Everything*. And if I believed that, I'd buy the swampland I'm sure you'd been selling while you were away. I'd also be a fool, which I am not, but I'll humor you. What exactly was 'everything' in your book?"

Kurt scowls, a rare outward sign of his waning patience with the woman he once called daughter. "Put the gun down and let's sit down and talk."

"I'm not ready to put the gun down," she replies. "I'm not sure I'll put it down until you're dead."

If he knows her, if he's paid her one ounce of attention all her life, he understands that the coldness in her, tells a story. She's not one to blow smoke. Ana shot me, but she never wanted me dead, but then Ana never saw me as the enemy. She does him.

# CHAPTER TWO

## ANA

I'd say I'm living in a twisted episode of *The Twilight Zone*, but the room echoes with lies.

With Kurt standing in front of me, my weapon aimed at him with the steady hand he trained me to maintain, his famous words ring in my mind: *Trusting is your choice. Proving you wrong is your enemy's decision.*

He not only made his decision, but he also has to live with it.

I went from elated to see the man I once considered my father, to ready to kill him in all of about thirty seconds. I can't trust him and I know this because he told me that the instant he held the gun at my head. Then he killed Parker and drove that point home. He's not here to protect me. He's here to protect himself and as he stands here before me, I swear to the good Lord above, he's going to tell me the truth of what's going on here. All of it.

"You sure you want to point that gun at me, Ana?" he challenges, his eyes calculating, as is his demeanor. If he was all about love and reconciliation, why is that what I read in him? No good reason, I'm certain.

Luke steps to my side, a silent source of support, who knows me well enough to know that I need this confrontation to be mine, just mine, at least for right now but I appreciate his presence. It's right, in ways Kurt's is not.

"I went to your funeral, Kurt," I remind him as if that says it all, and it does. His very presence defines his death as a lie. It also sends a message. The past died with him, and that past included me.

"Some people might suggest you should be happy I'm alive," he replies.

"Unless you tell me you've been held prisoner for three years and just escaped, I'm going to assume you washed your hands of me and everything in your life, and only showed back up because you need something."

His jaw tics. "All right. You want to do it this way, then we'll do it this way. Here are the cold hard facts, baby girl. I had a good life. You have a good life. Kasey fucked that up. He got involved with the wrong people. He owed them money. The only way I could save him was to agree to do a job for them."

"Who is *them?*" Luke asks, echoing the question that's in my mind.

Kurt continues as if Luke hasn't spoken, "One job turned into another job and another. You would have eventually gotten pulled into it. You were their leverage. I had to work for them to protect you."

I grimace at the ridiculousness of that reply. "Aside from the fact that you would never, ever allow someone to intimidate you into disappearing," I state, "what happened to working for them to protect Kasey?"

"Kasey stopped being my son long before he died. These people are not stupid. They knew I was going to walk away from them and him."

He speaks those words with the kind of icy certainty that would cool off hell and tells me more than I ever wanted to know about Kurt. Because I'd idolized the person who'd raised me, in blind and stupid ways that didn't allow me to see the real man.

"Then he was never your son," I state, a fact, not a question. "And I'm not your daughter."

"You are *not* Kasey, Ana," he assures me, an irritated twitch to his jaw as if I'm the one being unreasonable right now. "You know that. You're a smart person, choosing to play dumb. You know what your brother was like."

He taught me to turn off the emotional switch, and never allow myself to be baited. I will not be baited now. "He was *your son*," I repeat.

"Don't even go down that bullshit path with me," he snaps. "I gave up *everything* for that boy, only to discover he'd happily hang me, and *you*, out to dry, to line his pockets. Even parents have limits." He holds up his hands. "I get it, though. You think I'm a cold-hearted bastard."

My lips press together and I fix him in a stare as cold as his behavior. Sometimes silence says more than a million words, another Kurt teaching, I know all too well. This is one of those times.

He gives me a deadpan stare, void of emotion, but there is a calculating quality to his mood.

Second tick by in which he seems to assess just how hard my code is to crack, before turning his efforts in another direction. He lifts his chin in Luke's direction. "I wasn't there the day you killed Kasey, but I know you. And I know for a fact that you tried to spare him, and did so to protect Ana. Kasey was another story. He didn't care about saving you. He cared about getting you out of his way. Even if that meant you had to die. Tell me I'm wrong."

"I find it interesting that you know that I was the one who killed him," Luke counters. "It was never in the news. Ana made sure of it. So how did you know?" He motions toward Parker's lifeless body. "Him?"

"He's one of them," Kurt replies, "one of the men after a treasure big enough to please their boss. He saw me as that prize. He would have told them I was alive, and then they would have come for me and Ana. And probably you. Kasey—"

"Is dead," I state flatly. "You *are not*. We need to know who these people are. Debating Kasey's personality and decisions gets us nowhere."

"And yet it does," he counters. "The jobs I was forced to take, just kept coming, right along with the threats against you, Ana. I couldn't find the head of the snake to cut it off. These people—they have no name that I've ever discovered—are well funded and well hidden."

"You have connections in the government," Luke reminds him. "Why not get help?"

"You think I didn't try? One phone call and my phone pinged with a photo of Ana and a promise there was a man with a gun on her. That's when I told Kasey it was time to disappear, to stage our deaths, to bury my money, so there was nothing for them to come for. That way all you represented to them was a badge and trouble."

I'm about to challenge him to prove any of this, preferably all of this, and actually, why the heck was Kasey present and accounted for when he was not if his story is true? Luke reads my mind and chimes in with that exact point. "Kasey didn't disappear when you did."

"He was supposed to," he replies. "When the time came, he double-crossed me. He no-showed to our exit zone. He left me no choice but to leave him behind and penniless."

"Why didn't he tell these people you were alive?" I challenge.

"I was involved because of him. Kasey would have been told to find me or die. And finding me wasn't going to pay the bills." His gaze latches onto mine. "I know you, Ana. Had I told you any of this, you would have worn this problem like an obligation your badge created. You would have tried to fix what cannot be fixed."

"Of course, it can be fixed," I snap. "Everything can be fixed."

"And therefore, you were obligated to make her suffer," Luke interjects, replying directly to Kurt. "Because she suffered, Kurt. She hurt. She literally heaved her guts out at the funeral."

He flicks Luke a look filled with condemnation. "She can handle it. She's tough."

*Don't put Baby in a corner.* Well, don't even think about putting *me* in a corner. Luke isn't having it. "What she *can* handle and what she *should have to* handle are two different things."

I reach out and catch Luke's arm, silently letting him know how much his presence means to me but also that I've got this. All of this is, after all, the price I pay for being blind and stupid until now, but no more. The idea that Kurt knows me, really knows me, and I clearly don't know him, is not just pathetic. It's potentially deadly when it involves a man who can spot weakness a mile away.

And as Kurt once told me—know how you are perceived and use it against your enemy.

I was dumb and stupid so he sees me as dumb and stupid.

I file that away in my mental information box.

At some point, even if it's not this moment, I'll use that against him.

And I'll use it against him as painfully as he used it against me.

**LISA RENEE JONES**

# CHAPTER THREE

## ANA

The emotional football Luke and I have played for days works against Kurt. I don't even like games. I'm done playing them with Luke. I'm not playing them with him. What I desire is the elusive thing called happiness, that I haven't known in the two years I've been apart from Luke. Now that he's back in my life, I don't intend to let either one of us die. That means I need answers, and it's answers I seek from Kurt now. I decide it's time to approach him not as my ex-stepfather because he is no one I will ever call family again, but rather as a witness.

Unfortunately, that means playing mental games. When it's put that way, perhaps, I like games more than I thought I did.

Now is the time for me to not only back him into a corner of his own making but to hold him there. That just happens to translate into me calling his bullshit and cornering him, to tell the truth. "Kasey was alive when you supposedly died," I remind him. "Surely, they, whoever *they* are, used me as leverage against him. That downgrades your story to a big, fat lie. You disappeared to protect yourself, not me."

"Leverage only works, honey, if the person cares about what's being leveraged. I'm not going to sugarcoat this, because that's not what you want from me or anybody. Kasey only cared about Kasey."

There it is. More emotional football.

Of course, I've come to terms with how little I meant to Kasey, but it doesn't seem to matter.

Kurt saying it, and saying it that brutally, jolts me clear to the soul.

He might as well have stabbed me in my bleeding, sisterly heart, but somehow, I manage to contain an outward reaction. My gaze is steady, and my hand steadier. I don't so much as blink. I don't take his bait and that's what it was, but I do return the favor. I bait him. "I'm back to the only thing in this conversation I know to be true. You ran. You hid. You were too scared to stand and fight."

His expression transforms into what I call his "angry bull face" normally reserved for combat drills. But then, perhaps this is the verbal version of just that. His lips pull tight, his jawline stretched, a tight knot of muscle bunched up just above his molars. "I didn't run or hide," he replies, and to his credit, despite his physical reaction, he manages a rather matter-of-fact tone.

"Ouch," I say. "Hit a nerve much? Come on, Kurt. You ran. You hid. Or you're lying. Which is it?"

In a poorly timed return, and just when I have Kurt where I want him, about to break, Adam reappears with a rope in hand. "We doing this or not?"

Kurt casts him a lazy, uninterested look that is anything but those things. He's assessing him, assessing the room. Trying to find a way to take control, which cannot happen. Not now. Not ever again. His attention turns to me, his expression cooled, his temper banked, his focus now razor-sharp on the one real obstacle in the room, which is me. If he wins me over, if he earns my trust, he wins the room.

"Everything I did, I did to protect you," he repeats softening his voice, ensuring it's for my ears only. "You *have* to know that."

I'm actually surprised at his return to the same thing, over and over.
*I'm protecting you, Ana.*
*I did it for you, Ana.*
He watches me for a reaction. My returned stare is a mix of bored and cynical, both of which he apparently reads as he abandons our connection, and turns his attention to Adam. "We're doing this," he says, in what appears to signal his acceptance of his failure, and retreat, at least for now. He cannot win me over.

Adam glances at me for the confirmation that I readily offer him. "Please tie him up but don't forget that he's a killer who trained people like Savage. No one, and I mean *no one*, is a better killer than Kurt."

Savage steps forward, all big and mighty, in that over-the-top Savage way of his, clears his throat, and in what I'm coming to know as his typical dopey self, predictably says, "I'm up for that challenge. Bring it big daddy bear. Let's get grisly."

My eyes meet Kurt's steely stare and I say, "Please don't make him kill you before I have the chance."

"I don't believe you'll kill me," Kurt replies. "I raised you. I'm your father."

He goes all in on the blast from the past, that was, from what I can tell, nothing but a lie in the first place.

"All you are to me right now is the man who lied to me and held a gun to my head. You might also be someone who has the answers I need. Maybe you'll decide to give them to me after you sit tied to a chair long enough." I start walking toward the kitchen where a stairwell leads to the second level of the house. I don't look back. He didn't, not until something forced him to do otherwise, and I absolutely believe that's what's happening right now.

He didn't choose to return. He was forced to return.

And if we don't find out why fast enough, we will all die.

And no matter what, we need to take Kurt's advice. In his own words, no matter who they are, if they give you a reason to believe they're the enemy, they're the enemy. Kurt's our enemy. We cannot forget that. That's when a realization hits me. I turned off the security system when we arrived to allow us to enter The Ranch. What if Kurt isn't alone? I dash toward the hallway behind the kitchen, cut right, and enter the security booth. With fast hands, I flip on the security system, movement alarms, and cameras. I stand there and scan the feed. Finally, I determine all is calm.

But it really does feel like the calm before the storm.

Or maybe I should say life before death.

And a new reality where Kurt lives and we all die.

# CHAPTER FOUR

## LUKE

I should follow Ana, I *will* follow Ana, but I'm not quite done with Kurt.

Ana was wrong about him being the best killer out there. Kurt never claimed to be the best. Kurt's special skill, his nasty little skill, is his ability to extract the man from the killer and therefore create a monster. He can smell weakness and manipulate it, and manifest it into something you don't recognize as you. I know because he did it to me. Manipulation is his ticket, and he punches with it at every human target in his path. Later, much later probably, I'm going to think about what that tells me, about everything he's now confessed, if anything.

For now, I just want the bastard tied up and Adam appears to be of the same mindset. He steps in front of Kurt. "Hands behind your back."

Kurt smirks, but is surprisingly compliant, doing as told, while Adam moves to his rear to get the job done.

I stand my ground, facing off with Kurt.

He smirks, appearing amused by my attention.

Everything about Kurt's life, death, and return, screams bomb about to explode. He needs to be secured, dominated by those ropes, and our team before I'll feel comfortable turning my back on him. Before I'll leave him alone with Adam and Savage.

"You know I spoke the truth," Kurt says, somehow turning his captivity into my captivity and putting his master manipulation to work. "About Kasey," he adds. "About Ana. About you leaving her to die."

I didn't fucking leave her to die.

My fingers curl in my palms, a tick forming in my left jaw. He's trying to trigger me, and he's not a complete failure, despite me knowing exactly what he's doing. What I *don't* know is what he thinks he's achieving right now. To stir guilt in me? My submission to that guilt and therefore him? Whatever the fuck, but that's not what he gets.

Yes, I feel like shit for leaving Ana, years of guilt fester inside me, but I'm back with Ana, and I'm here to stay. If we believe his story, the cesspool of danger and bullshit that created my departure, and Ana's heartache, came from his decision to leave us in the dark over Kasey. The suffering she endured could have been avoided had I simply not taken Kasey with me on that mission. And I wouldn't have. Not if I'd known he was dirty.

Damn Kurt to hell, where he should have crawled and stayed. As if proving that point, anger explodes inside me, and I do what I would never do if I was in my right mind. I step up on an unarmed man with his hands tied behind his back and punch the hell out of him. His head snaps back. Blood gushing from the left side of his lower lip.

It was a pussy move on my part, and for what? I don't feel better.

Fuck.

I want to do it again. I turn away from him and start walking before I do that and more.

He reads me like a book and calls out, "Feel better, son?"

I halt and turn back to him. "I wish like hell that was all it took to make me feel better, you smug prick. Had I known what I know now, Kasey might be alive and I would never have left Ana's side."

"Holy hell, I taught you better than this. Emotion kills so for God's sake, stop wallowing in guilt and the blood of what can't be changed because that shit will get you and Ana killed. As for Kasey. Kasey got Kasey killed. As for you and Ana, you chose to leave and kill what you had with her. Punch me all you want but that's not on me."

"Spoken like a man who never takes accountability for a problem. He just kills them off."

"As you said, if only it was that simple, this problem would be dead right now."

My mind jerks back in time, to the day, a long time ago, when I met Kurt, a day I told Ana about but left out details. Not because I was hiding things from her, but because it wasn't the kind of memory any of us hold onto. I was in Saudi Arabia, of all places considering that's where Kasey died, and I can almost feel the muggy, stifling hot night, suffocating me.

My team of six had been on a mission to protect innocents from a hostile, when Kurt and his team had landed in our path, on the same side of right versus wrong. Only right felt pretty damn wrong when Kurt had killed a kid, not more than sixteen, and did so to save my life. The kid meant to kill me, he did, and I got that, but I suffered over that kill while Kurt lost not a second of his life to regret or guilt. "Kill or be killed, son," he'd said to me, later that night. "Keep it simple. Leave the emotion out of the kill."

And Lord, help me, that's what I did. Too often, too many times, until one day, until—until some bad shit happened. The kind of shit a man struggles to come back from. I wasn't sure I'd ever like the man in the mirror again. But Ana did, and that was all I needed. After I killed Kasey, I didn't think she could like that man again. And so, I left. Or maybe I ran.

She saved me and I haven't done near enough to save her.

I forget about Kurt, and exit the room, leaving him behind, and seeking out Ana, because while she can do anything on her own, when I asked her to be my wife and she said yes, we made a pact. We said we were better off together and I believed that then, just as I do now. She needed me in the past. She's always needed me, even after I became the man who killed her brother.

I round the corner and enter the kitchen to find Ana standing there, and I stop short, certain she's heard everything that happened between me and Kurt. I'm sure she did. She had to have. I'm not sure what I expect to find in her reaction, but what I do discover is uncertainty in her and a sense of awkwardness that shreds me. Because I know where those feelings come from. I know how it feels to have your world pulled out from under you, to have everything you thought you knew, no longer be true. Because that's how I felt that day at the funeral, when I showed up for Ana, even after she shot me—and back then I thought she meant to shoot me—and she still hated me.

I belonged nowhere.

And right now, she thinks she belongs nowhere.

She doesn't even know she belongs with me.

My hands come down on her upper arms, and drag her to me, her soft curves flush with my body when I say just that. "You belong with me, Ana, and you have from the moment we met. And I belong with you." I kiss her hard and fast or that's my intent.

I seem to have hit on exactly what she needed to hear and feel right now.

Because she melts into me, her arms hooking under my shoulders, her breasts pressed to my chest, and her mouth against mine, a desperation that bleeds into me, feeds more of the same in me. I cup her head, deepening the kiss, drink her in, and feel the pull of hunger inside and between us that defies our circumstances because it's about loss. And there's just too much fucking loss in our lives right now. I swear I'd carry her someplace private and bury myself inside her if it weren't for one icy reality. Kurt might be a distraction, with an attack to follow.

With agonizing effort, I tear my lips from hers, and say, "The security system."

"It's on. We're all clear."

Any relief I feel from this news is my certainty none of this ends until things get bloody. All the more reason I need to be right with Ana. "Then we need to go somewhere we can be alone, baby."

She nods and pushes out of my arms, wetting her lips with her delicate little tongue, before she rotates and is already moving toward the stairs that lead to the master bedroom.

**LISA RENEE JONES**

# CHAPTER FIVE

## LUKE

I pursue Ana with a sense of momentary comfort with the safety of our surroundings.

The security system is on, Kurt is tied up and guarded by two trusted, skilled friends, and our enemies, at least some of them, have given us three more days to deliver the package. A package I don't have. That's a mountain I must climb, a problem I must dissect, but for now, Ana is my focus.

Ana is everything.

With her shoulders back, she charges ahead, and I decide that despite all the things I could say to her, about the past and the future, wanting a future with her, it all comes back to actions, being present, being by her side, understanding what she needs from me. I can't know what that means if I don't show up, and I don't ask. But I'm here now, and it felt as if we were headed toward the light at the end of the dark tunnel.

Until now.

Until Kurt's return.

He's shifted the mood, and with his presence, there's a distinct uncertainty in the air, about our lives and our futures. Because if nothing was as it seems, how can we possibly know what is real?

I feel that. Ana has to be feeling it magnified by a hundred.

And while I know I should be happy for Ana's reconnection with Kurt, nothing about his presence feels right. It's as if the ground opened up and a sword rose from the deepest depths of the ground, waiting for us to fall upon it and die.

Ana will not die. On the Lord above, I swear I will be the sword that protects her.

The way Kurt's return tests the delicate bond we've sewn, stirs possessiveness inside me. With it, the wholly male side of me burns to reclaim her in every possible way, before Kurt somehow rips her out of my arms and my life. I'm aware of her body, the sweet sway of her hips, aware of how damn much I want to kiss her again, touch her again. Talk is messy. And not the right kind of messy.

Ana reaches the upper level of the house and disappears out of my view. I'm a couple of seconds behind her, following her into the master bedroom that once was Kurt's, and later Kasey's. She's never called it her own, declaring it cursed, as everyone who claimed it, died, or at least pretended to die, in Kurt's case. But the room was never cursed. Actions lead to reactions. And if we believe Kurt, Kasey's actions fucked us all.

I don't believe Kurt on much right now, but it's a little too easy to use Kasey as a fall guy.

This is why me and Ana need to get right with each other.

All in.

That's the ending to this story.

Me. Her. Married.

Fuck the rest of the world.

# CHAPTER SIX

## ANA

I stand in the center of the room that was once Kurt's, and later Kasey's, but never mine. It's cursed, or so I thought it was if you believe in such things, because everyone who claimed it as their own ended up dead, only Kurt wasn't dead. He lied. It's a thought I can't get off repeat in my head.
*He's not dead.*
*He lied.*
All of it was a lie.
I'm on mental repeat, but with good reason. I need his betrayal cemented in my mind. No matter how connected I feel to Kurt, the man I called my only living parent before he "died," the lie he told was a brutal lie and one that speaks of no confidence in my abilities and decision-making.
He didn't trust me not to get killed.
If I was that incompetent, I shouldn't wear a badge.
Or he just wanted to get rid of me. I can't know which or what combination of all the above comes into play. Because he's a liar. If he were Pinocchio, his nose would be too long for him to deny the truth.
I forget that thought, and easily, for one good reason: Luke walks into the room and in this moment, I am struck by how beautiful he is, and I know that would seem crazy to most people considering what is happening in my life at present. But he's my person, the man I love, the one human being I know would never betray me. This point has been driven home more in the past few days than I ever thought possible. I'm just

glad I realized that long before Kurt showed back up because Luke, more than ever, needs to know that I'm present and accounted for, and it has nothing to do with everyone else betraying me.

Right now is about him. And us. It's about everything we've ever shared, and all the things I want to share with him in the future. And I do want a future with Luke. I also heard parts of what happened downstairs, which is why I wait for him to shut the door before I say, "I don't need you to take care of me. I can take care of myself. So, his bullshit guilt-inducing blubber he's spewing on you needs to go in one ear and out the other. And what the hell is this, Luke? I went to his funeral. I can't be happy he's alive and Lord help me, I don't mean that how it came out. Okay, maybe I do. I really *want* to kill him right now."

He's already in front of me, big and tall. And strong, mentally and physically. He's actually stronger than I will ever be when he'd say the opposite. He'd tell me I'm the strong one. He'd tell me I make him stronger. And better. But it's me who is stronger with him. Me who is better with him.

His fingers tangle in my hair and he tilts my gaze to his, as he declares, "Screw Kurt and the horse he rode in on," the rough quality of his voice sending a shiver up and down my spine and I swear the heat of his body burns through me. My fingers curl around his shirt, holding onto him in any way I can hold onto him as he adds, "*You* have nothing to feel guilty for. Think about it, Ana. What does it say about Kurt, that we both had to say that to each other?"

"I know," I whisper. "I'm just confused right now."

"You feel what you feel because he made you feel it and he's not stupid. He knows that. He *knows*. And it works in his favor, be it simply a way to get you to accept him again, or a way to distract us from whatever he has on his agenda. He has a lot to explain."

"He did explain," I say, a pinch in my chest that might as well be a blade. "At least for my part, he told me everything I need to know. He disowned Kasey. We both know he did the same to me."

"I don't believe that's what's happening, baby," he says, his thumb stroking my cheek, and it's funny how little things like a gentle caress and an endearment mean so much in such uncertain times.

"Then what is happening?" I ask, covering his hand with mine.

"I don't know, but at least right now, I'll say it again, screw Kurt. You're what matters. You're my *everything*, Ana. You know that, right? I *cannot* lose you again."

I'd tell him I feel the same. I'd tell him how much I need him and how thankful I am that he's here now, but I never get the chance. His mouth slants over my mouth. And then he's kissing me again, and it's not the tentative, trying-to-hold-back kiss he'd offered me downstairs. No, this kiss is different. It's possessive, greedy even, a fierce addictive demand of his tongue, that is as seductive as it is impossible to resist. This is what I need. *He* is what I need right now.

I lean into him, press to my toes, and reach for any and every part of him I can manage to touch. Touching him is as addictive as the kiss and I can't get enough of his sinewy muscle beneath my hands. I want him naked, but somehow that feels too complicated, and everything is just so damn complicated right now. I slide my hand down the front of his jeans and press my palm to the thick bulge of his erection against his zipper.

A low, gruff sound escapes his lips and he lifts me and carries me toward the bathroom, which I suspect is because the lock on the door of the bedroom is broken and we are about to be naked and not soon enough. He sets me down, his hands sliding under my shirt, his fingers roughly teasing my nipples. I moan against the sensation, and his mouth on my mouth, drinking in the sound, drinking in me. I've had moments in my time with Luke when I've been desperate for him, but this time is different. This time it feels like everything we are together is on the line and I don't know why. He is here. I am here. We both want to be here.

Maybe it's the realization that we were never in control. We never chose to travel the path that divided us. Everyone else did, and one of those people is tied up downstairs. Someone I should be happy to see, but for reasons I can't explain, that reach deeper than his lies, that's not what I feel. I don't know what I feel.

And I'm thinking too much.

Luke handles that though. God does he. He drags my shirt over my head, and my bra is gone in seconds. Already he's leaning in, suckling my nipples, sending waves of pleasure through me. My fingers dive into his hair, twisting, and not gently. His mouth is not gentle either. He suckles me to the point of pain that is an absolute pleasure. How does he know exactly what to do? How does he get everything so right? My sex clenches, and I am so wet, it's almost embarrassing, an intense throb between my legs, where I need him nice and hard and buried deep right now. Because that's what I want. Him inside me. Me lost in every thrust and pump of his body. *Lost in him.* Connected to him, so much so that there is room for nothing but him. I reach for his pants again, impatient for him, God, I need him. He cups my face and tilts my gaze to his. "Say it, Ana."

"Which part? I love you or please fuck me?"

His eyes glow with male satisfaction, which I love, as much as I do him. Because that look in his eyes means he's the kind of animal I need right now. "Fuck me, *please*," I repeat.

He kisses me, biting my lips, pinching my nipples and it's a brutal, sweet perfection. I'm panting when his lips part mine, and he turns me to face the sink forcing me to catch my hands on the counter. I'd complain about not being able to touch him, but he's touching me, and that makes up for it. His eyes meet mine in the mirror, and he watches me as he plays with my hard, puckered nipples, my teeth worrying my lip, eyes fluttering. But even when they shut, I can feel his hot, hungry stare, feel his lust and desire.

And it's such a turn-on.

His palms caress down my body, leaving my nipples cold and aching when they had been on fire only moments before. His teeth scrape my neck, his hands press under the cotton of my leggings and drag them down. I toe off my shoes, and he lifts me, tugging away my clothing. But there's no time to process how naked I am while he is not. He steps to my right, his legs in front and behind my leg, and reaches around with one hand and drags my mouth to his, while his other hand slides down my belly and two fingers press inside my sex.

"Oh God," I murmur against his lips. "God. Luke, I—Please." It's a desperate plea, but his fingers, they're relentless, demanding I press against them, pump against their movement, and I don't want to come like this. But I might. I really, really think I will.

Soon.
Now.
No.

He drags his fingers out of me, and I gasp, only to realize that he's shoving his pants down.

Moments later, that feel like a lifetime, he's lifting my leg, anchoring my hips to his hips, and pressing inside me, thrusting deep, and hard, his cock thick as it settles in, all intimate and right. And then he's shackling my hips, thrusting, and thrusting, a frenzied rhythm to the way he pumps inside me, rubbing me all the right ways, inside and out. I'm so close to the edge again, but it's so far away, and I like it like that.

Harder.

Just fuck me harder.

I don't want this to end.

When he pulls out and turns me around, kissing me all dirty and messy, and shoves his fingers in my mouth even as he pushes his cock inside me, all I can breathe out is, "Yes." I don't even know what the question is. But the answer is yes.

I suck on his fingers, and he pushes deeper inside me, lifts me, anchors me on the counter, and just grinds with me. His eyes are all over my breasts, watching them sway and bounce, and again, I just whisper, "Yes." He never asks what "yes" means.

Yes, is pretty clear.

Keep doing what you're doing and do more of it.

Eventually more is too much, or not enough, however, you want to look at being driven to the most intense orgasm of your life. My body quakes and jerks, and it's like this earthquake erupting in my body. I take him with me too, drag him to the point of no return, but how can he not come with me? My sex is spasming so hard, that his cock never has a chance of holding back.

He shudders and roars out this guttural reaction, that is as primal as it is hot.

We crash into each other, melt there, me on the sink, and him holding me, neither of us speaking. Perhaps because we both know when we do, the rest of the world matters. And the rest of the world is going to scream loudly to be heard. It's already screaming in my head and I don't like anything it says. Yet I know I have to listen. And so does Luke.

We break apart, staring at each other, that understanding in our shared look.

But there's also another understanding.

One that says we both needed this. We both need each other. He grabs a towel and presses it between my legs, and then rights his pants. My gaze lowers and lands on his hand where it rests on my leg, a bloody cut on top. I catch his fingers. "What happened?"

His blue eyes burn with shame. "I punched him."

"I wanted to punch him. He deserved it."

"He was tied up Ana, which I'm not proud of."

Honesty.

That's how I see his confession. He was honest, despite how he felt that might affect my narrative about him. "Why did you punch him?" I ask, which seems to me to be the real way to define a bitch move, as he calls it.

"He made you go to his funeral and then held a gun to your head, Ana. I was scared shitless I was going to your funeral. And I swear to you, he would not have lived to see that day."

My heart swells all over again, emotions trembling in my belly. "How am I supposed to be angry with you when you were just protecting me, Luke?"

"Punching a man who's tied up is not protecting you."

"You forget that you're the one who held a gun on him when he was holding one to me. He sucker punched us with the funeral and used me as a shield. He deserved to be punched, Luke. How can you think I'd look down on you for protecting me and my honor?"

"I thought you didn't want to be protected?"

"That's the thing about being protected when you can protect yourself. It still feels good." Those emotions in my belly now burn my chest. "Fuck Kurt," I whisper.

Luke slides a hand over my hair and tilts my face to his, but he doesn't say "Fuck Kurt." "We both needed to say those words, baby, but they won't solve our problems. As much as I want it to be that simple, it's not. We have to face this, whatever the hell this is, and get as dirty as we have to get to make our happily ever after, and it won't be the good kind of dirty."

He's right.

It won't be the good kind of dirty.

In fact, this is all a little too dirty, in all the wrong ways.

# CHAPTER SEVEN

## ANA

He's right.
Everything is just so damn dirty right now.
Suddenly *I feel* dirty. And other things I don't quite understand.
I don't like it.
"I need down off this counter. I need to get dressed. And why is this bathroom so small? It's the master."
He catches my waist and sets me on the ground, but he doesn't let me go, he doesn't step away. His powerful legs frame my legs, the roughness of his jeans pressed to my bare skin. I'm suddenly aware of my state of nakedness. His state of being fully dressed.
"What just happened?" his hands settling warmly on my hips.
"We have to get back to work. You just said that. And you're not even undressed. I feel—I don't like how I feel right this second."
"Baby, it just happened."
"I get that. I do. I have no idea why it bothers me right now, but it does." Only I do, I decide silently. I'm reacting to a sense of unease that's rapidly becoming a crushing sensation, like I'm being buried alive in all that dirtiness he spoke of.
And our breakup is part of that dirtiness. It doesn't matter that it was a product of everyone else's dirtiness. It became ours. And I learned how to deal with everyone I loved being gone. Now two of the most recently lost, are back.
It's confusing.

I'm not sure if I should be celebrating or protecting myself.

What if they leave again? What if *Luke* leaves again?

He stares down at me with his dreamy, blue, angelic eyes. The kind of stunning eyes one would imagine the Archangel Michael possesses, eyes that could seduce you, only to cast you to hell forever more.

"I was impatient, Ana," he assures me. "You do that to me. Being without you for so long does that to me."

Really, truly, those eyes and that deep, baritone voice of his, is pure seduction and there's no saving me from whatever he cast upon me. There's really no reason to hide that from him. It's not like I'm going to fight it, but I still need a little space to deal with that realization. "I just need to be dressed right now," I say. "It's a control thing. I know you know me well enough to know that."

"And then you'll talk about what's really wrong?"

"Maybe."

I don't know how it's possible, but his blue eyes darken to a deeper blue. He studies me for several intense seconds, the muscle in his jaw flexing, resistance in his energy, but he gives a forced nod, backing up to allow me space. Once committed to obeying my request for space, he goes one step further. He doesn't leave, but he sets the toilet seat down before he sits, facing the wall, rather than watching me struggle with my clothes. That's the thing about Luke. He's a dominant personality, but he's also confident enough to not force his dominance down anyone's throat. I need space, a little, not a lot, and he seems to understand.

And he didn't leave.

Almost as if he sensed that his leaving was where my head was at right then. I'm afraid of getting hurt again. And no one but Luke could hurt me to the point of devastation. And while not exactly the same dynamic, I can say, not even Kurt.

Once I'm fully clothed again, he pushes to his feet and almost as if he's been sitting there waiting for this moment, he catches me to him again, backs me against the door and cups my face. He does that a lot. I like it a lot. Maybe too much if we don't end up together.

"I want to say so many things right now, Ana," he murmurs, his voice rough like sandpaper. "But we have a lifetime for me to say them. The minute we have the chance, we're making this official. I'm going to whisk you away and put that ring on your finger anywhere, anyway, you want to do it."

Everything inside me softens, the tension I'd felt moments before fading away. My hand settles on his chest. "I won't kid you and tell you I'm not afraid this ends with us apart, but it's not what I want. When this is over—"

"Soon," he promises.

"I hope so. I mean why is Kurt back now? Why not when Kasey died?"

Luke releases me and scrubs his jaw, pressing his hands to his waist. "Okay let's think about this. He made me promise to take care of you." When I would object, he holds up a hand, "Hear me out, baby. Those are not the words of a man who wrote you off, but as I think back to that day, it is a man who knew something was coming long before it came."

I think back to that day, or night actually, that he's referencing. To the first time I'd taken Luke to dinner at my father's place as my date. Kasey was there, too, and while my father had been welcoming, everything with Kasey had been combative. But it was Kurt, who'd called Luke "Lucifer" so many times that I'd finally lost my patience.

"*Luke,*" I'd corrected. "His name is *Luke.*"

My brother's reply had been one of his famous smartass snorts. "Like the name erases Lucifer from his blood. You really think if we call him Luke, we erase every reason he earned that nickname?"

It had been a whole thing that had led Luke to confess some things about his past to me, he'd feared sharing. But I'd found him vulnerable and honest.

I blink to the real memory he's referencing.

Kurt had met us at the door when we'd arrived for dinner and I slip back into that memory, right after the two men had shaken hands.

*Kurt meets Luke's stare, and says, "You know what I like about you?"*

*"I used to think it was my ability to do my job, sir," is Luke's reply, of course, referencing his combat and aviation skills, which Kurt often references as "exceptional."*

*"It still is," Kurt assures him. "And at some point, if my daughter decides you're a keeper, one day, when I'm no longer around, your job will be to protect her."*

*Frustrated with the direction of the conversation, I quickly say, "I can take care of myself," but I don't miss how Kurt's eyes meet Luke's, a challenge in their depths.*

I blink back to the present and funny how I'd seen that moment differently. At the time, I'd just thought Kurt was overplaying the protective father, and while a bit irritating, still rather charming the way it played out, on both their parts. Now I'm not sure I read it right at all. "He knew something was coming but we didn't," I say. "Maybe. If that's true though, how do we know that anything with Kurt was ever real? We clearly missed a lot of things going on around us."

"I thought the same thing at first, but let's be logical not emotional. We weren't at The Ranch or involved with Kurt and Kasey on a daily basis before Kurt died. We were living our own lives. I was overseas and you were involved in your work."

I wave off that answer. He's trying to make me feel better. I don't want to feel better. I want this to end and it ends because we face the facts. "That's an excuse we both know we aren't willing to accept," I say. "We were at The Ranch after Kurt died. We were around Kasey."

"And we both knew nothing about Kasey was ever right. You tried to help him after Kurt disappeared but it's more obvious than ever, he didn't want to be saved."

"He didn't want to die, either," I argue. "That's not what he wanted."

It's the wrong thing to say. It's completely *not* the right thing to say, but it's out before I can stop it, words that flew from my mouth, fueled by emotion.

His jaw is an instant band, pulled tight and hard, the air chilled and when he exits the bathroom, I'm reaching for him. He's too fast. He escapes but not for long. I'm not done with this conversation that isn't what he believes it to be at all. But the very fact that he believes it to be, tells me we're still broken.

The glass half full has not only been knocked to the ground. It's shattered and empty.

**LISA RENEE JONES**

# CHAPTER EIGHT

## LUKE

I'm headed for the bedroom door with the roar of my own voice in my head. *Who the fuck am I kidding with all this happily-ever-after marriage bullshit?*

I killed her brother. Why the hell do I think she will actually marry me? Yet, in what is clearly a ridiculous point of view, I've convinced myself that's doable. I can marry Ana. I can live the dream. As if I didn't fucking pull that trigger. As if anyone could live with that kind of baggage. A load and a half that would exist every day for the rest of our lives. I don't know how I live with the pain in her eyes. I don't know how she lives with the man responsible for her brother's death, no matter what led to the ultimate act. I don't know how the hell we do any of that. I also don't know how the hell to live without her. I don't fucking know how. I've been miserable alone.

Alone even when I was with other people. Even other women. No one could make me forget her and fuck knows I've tried. Because she hated me. Because on some level she still does or those words would not have come out of her mouth just now.

I'm ready to exit the room and clear my head when Ana steps between me and my exit, her hands pressed to my chest. I hate how damn good it feels to have her touch me even when she just called me a killer. A brother killer. The worst of the killers out there. Except maybe a baby killer. Thank fuck there is still a low I haven't reached.

"That wasn't about you, Luke," she promises, "and I hate that you think it was. I hate that is where we're still at right now. I'm sorry."

"I don't think anything, Ana. You said the words. *He didn't want to die.* You might as well have said, you didn't have to kill him. And yet, I did. Because I wanted to live. And I wanted the woman he was holding a gun to her head, to live. I guess it is what it is. We can't turn back time and change the outcome. Not that I can think of one thing I could have done differently that day. And believe me, I've tried."

"But we can understand it and accept it and I do. You're still looking for my blame that doesn't exist. I was talking about Kurt setting him up to die. You would never have had to kill Kasey if Kurt would have told us what was going on. Or at least, you. He could have told you."

She wasn't talking about me.

I don't even know what to do with that piece of information, but she means it. I see it in her eyes. I feel it in her energy. My shoulders soften and flex forward, the edge of my mood, notches downward but I'm still shaken by what I'd believed she meant. Her blame might not be present, but my own is alive and well, but I shove it aside and focus on the moment. On the present hellish twist of events that back us into a corner in a room that is not of our making. But then, none of this ever has been of our making.

None of it.

"I told him that," I say. "I told him he should have told me. It's what made me punch him. Had he told me, I would never have ended up where it was me and Kasey, and a life-or-death situation."

"Exactly my point," she says easily, but her tone is far from easy at all. It's raspy with emotion, tormented with both the past and the present that the past created. "And he said what to that?"

"That I would have told you. *I would have told you, Ana,*" I confirm. "You don't want him to be right about this because it doesn't support him keeping his secret. But for the record, the alternative means *I would have* kept a bombshell secret from you and let you suffer thinking he was dead. You have to know he's right on at least this. I would never have been able to do that."

Her lashes lower with what I am certain is the emotional rollercoaster of all this bullshit we're going through, and I steel myself for her reaction. But when she looks at me again, her voice softens. "I'm sorry. You're right. I don't like the alternative. Not at all. I hate we're going at each other."

My hands come down on her shoulders and I drag her delicate curves against me. "We're going to be okay," I promise, kneading the tension in her spine. "We'll find a way."

Her blue eyes spark with concern. "And if we don't?"

"That's not an option. We tried that. It was pretty fucking miserable for my part."

"Mine too," she assures me, her blue eyes turning all dewy and soft. "I like me better with you."

I stroke hair from her face. "I like me better with you, too, baby which is why we need to be objective about who Kurt is and what he's doing here. We might not like his methods, or the way he went about this, but there's a chance his intentions were honorable. You know that, right?"

She reaches up and touches my face, the tenderness in her expression transforming into something I can only call cold and bitter. "Don't want it too badly," she warns. "He'll use that against you and you'll end up dead instead of him. And that's not what I want. I choose you over Kurt. I always chose you, Luke." Her fingers curl around my shirt. "I don't know how to make you see that, either."

"Time, baby. We just need time and that time needs to be a whole hell of a lot more normal than where we're at now."

"And that will do it? That will be enough? Because it doesn't feel like it will be."

No, I think. It doesn't but we're going to make it enough. "We'll make it enough," I promise her, stroking her cheek.

We just look at each other, as if we both know, I'm speaking the impossible, but we both refuse to accept failure. She steps into me and I cup her face. "What if we can't?" she asks again.

"*We'll make it enough*," I vow, and then I kiss her because a kiss is so much simpler than words.

And maybe that's the answer I'm looking for. Keep it simple. Get us out of this mess and then fly her someplace exotic where we can stay naked for days on end. If we're naked, we can't fight. If she's moaning, she can't cry. If she's crying out my name, she can't call me other nastier names.

We'll fuck away the past.

I've almost convinced myself it really is that simple when there's a knock on the door and it's already opening. The past isn't done with us yet. Maybe it never will be.

# CHAPTER NINE

## ANA

With the door to the bedroom opening, Luke reaches for his weapon, clearly, in the same mindset I'm in, which is to expect a monster not a man. Kurt would be that monster. For just a moment, terror rips through me at the idea that Kurt has killed Adam and Savage while we got dirty in the bathroom.

Turns out there is no monster. It's only Adam.

Luke grunts and his hand slides away from his weapon, the steel arch of his back softening, if only a pinch, while my shoulders slump forward in relief.

Adam steps into the doorway, stone-faced, and tense, but clearly not as tense as me after I started seeing the walking dead, and found a monster in the man I once called my stepfather. I was also ready to call me and Luke insanely irresponsible for assuming safety that might not exist. We really don't know what is going on around us. Then again, we don't know how long we'll be alive at this point either, and sometimes you have to live in the moment.

"What the hell is going on?" he asks and he's looking at me as if I hold the knowledge to a universe where dead men start walking. If only I held that kind of golden information, none of us would still be in this house.

"I thought he was dead," I confirm, reading his complete exasperation as his assumption this surprise was not a surprise to me, but perhaps, only a betrayal. As if any betrayal is *only* a betrayal. It was both.

"She thought he was dead," Luke chimes in, offering me back up.

"I get that," Adam replies. "What I don't get is *what the hell is going on?*" He eyes Luke. "The rope was kinked. He wasn't tied up until after you left the room."

Obviously, that's code for—he wasn't tied up when you hit him—his way of saying that without saying it to protect Luke's reputation with me, which doesn't need protecting.

I meant it when I told Luke I wanted to hit Kurt. I wanted to shake him. I wanted him to just be a good man, who did the right things, but it's hard to believe he can be that person after a gun to my head and a pile of lies that now define my life. And my breakup with Luke.

Luke's eyes narrow with this information, his fingers flexing and curling on his dominant right hand. "He chose not to fight me."

"Don't go thinking that's an honor thing, Luke," I warn. "You know Kurt. This is a combat situation to him, and for all practical purposes, he's the hostile. And we both know he does nothing without an agenda." I glance at Adam. "Did you ask him why he didn't fight back?"

"I did," Adam confirms. "And he said it was to test Luke." His gaze flicks to Luke with that tidbit of information, as if he's watching him for impact. "He said you're a man of control. He made you hit him to prove a point. He wanted to know if you still cared about her enough to lose that control."

Luke gives a dry, humorless laugh. "He made me. Priceless. That's how he wants to play that hand?"

My lips press together and there's a splinter of ice down my spine. "He wanted to know if I was still your weakness. And I am. In other words, he wanted to know how to control Luke, and controlling Luke might as well be controlling all of us. Now we have to decide why he needed that information and how he intends to use it against us." I start walking toward the door.

Luke catches my arm and turns me to face him. "What are you doing?"

"I'm the one playing games, punishing him by having him tied up. That's just wasting time. We need answers. We aren't going to get them with him down there, and us up here."

"Tying him up wasn't a game," he says. "It was smart. It was your instinct and you cannot go down there thinking any differently, you hear me?"

I bristle, my defenses all kinds of prickly. "I don't need you to dictate to me how to handle myself or Kurt."

"If you don't think tying him up was a game," Adam replies from behind me, "he damn sure does."

I jerk out of Luke's grip and whirl around to face him again. "You don't know me well enough to go there."

"I consider Luke a brother. I would die for you, Ana. So yes, I know you well enough to speak up if it saves your life and his. Every action you took downstairs, was on the money. It was soldier mode. What you're doing right now, that's about emotion, which is human, but also dangerous. He's counting on that emotion as a weapon and one he tested on Luke."

"And I gave him my trigger," Luke replies dryly.

"You saved his life, man," Adam replies. "Had you challenged him properly you might have killed him. On some level, you knew that. He knew, too. And you also knew that would be the final wedge between you and Ana."

In my mind, I vehemently yearn to declare any wedge between me and Luke impossible, but I've already had similar thoughts to those expressed by Adam. The truth is that the bond between me and Luke is fragile at best, and neither of us would be speaking the truth if we said differently. Only I'm not sure if this is a together or apart kind of thing for us anymore. It feels more like we're holding onto each other, trying to walk a balance beam made for one, and doing so above a stormy, shark-infested sea. One move left or right, and we won't be divided. We'll just be dead.

# CHAPTER TEN

## ANA

*Believe or you will not achieve.*
Kurt didn't tell me this. My high school dance instructor did when I did a solo dance for regionals and was terrified because Kurt was going to be in the audience. Yes, I was on the dance team. A lot of people find that hard to believe, including Kurt. But I wanted to be a girl. I wanted to feel normal, but I learned that everyone's version of normal is different. Normal really just has to mean happy. And I'm happy when I'm sharing my life with Luke.

So, I focus on how I find my version of happy again. I focus not on how any of this might divide me and Luke, but on how ending it brings us back together. *Kurt is a manipulator*, I think again. Of all the weapons he handles with masterful skill, it's the one he uses to inflict the most damage.

"We can't let him use us against us. He's reading us like books and he'll use it all against us. That's the bottom line. We have to shift that narrative."

"I believe that to be a valid assessment," Adam replies. "Which is why I'm going to point out that we're in *his house* which we all know is a booby-trapped nightmare for those who are his enemies. Right now, we're his enemies. For all we know he's been here, living here, under your nose, Ana. This place is huge."

Luke casts me a questioning glance. I give a short nod. "It's possible," I agree. "I'm rarely here."

"Then he could have set us up for an attack," Adam continues. "Even if that's not the case, he has the upper hand here. We need to get him out of his comfort zone. We need to get off this ranch."

"The security system is state of the art," I reply. "And I made sure it's on."

"He was here when we got here," he reminds us. "Who else was here, meaning on the property, before we got here?"

"There are motion sensors for every region of the property," I reply. "I set it up on the highest alert. Right now, if there is movement in any region an entire house alarm alerts us. If I had my phone, it would be sent to my phone."

"Alarm or no alarm," Luke chimes in, "if there were enough men, positioned at the right places and they all moved at once, we'd be screwed. Adam's right. We're in his house, Ana, on his land. No one knows this place better than him. And if he's been living here, which is possible, who knows what kind of overrides he set-up to that security that could bite us in the ass. We need to get off this property."

"What if the trigger for an attack is us leaving?" I ask.

Adam scrubs his jaw and settles his hands on his hips. "She makes a point. I need to call Blake. He needs to take a look at the satellite images and the security system."

My mind races, filling with one moment, after another with Kurt, all of which guide me to my next conclusion. "He wouldn't allow himself to be tied up if we were about to be attacked. He could get caught in the crossfire."

"He didn't exactly allow it to happen," Adam replies.

"We didn't surprise him," I argue. "He was waiting for us."

"We don't know that," Adam counters.

"I do," I say. "He was waiting for us."

"In that realm of thinking," Adam presses, "are we really saying we didn't surprise him but Parker did?"

"Unless he didn't," Luke contemplates. "I'm guessing here, but somehow Kurt found out about our meeting, probably because Parker told his people, whoever they are. And Kurt had an inside man who leaked it to him."

"It makes sense," I agree. "He expected Parker. Parker didn't expect him. Parker was a problem he knew he'd end. Which he did. And we can speculate all day long on all of this but it's just that—speculation. I need to talk to Kurt." I hold up a hand to both of their impending objections. "I'm always the soldier he made me, more so now than when I was downstairs, reeling from his appearance and the gun he held to my head. And I strongly believe that before we make a move, I need to feel him out in a way only I can do. I'm ready to do that now."

Luke steps closer and in doing so lends his support for my decision. "I'll go with you."

I rotate and press my hand to his chest, holding him in place. "It needs to be me and him."

"I'll stay in the kitchen, Ana, within arm's reach, but I won't leave you alone with him."

"I can live with that." I try to pull my hand away.

His long fingers curl around my forearm and he steps into me. "He wants something, Ana." His voice is low, a foreboding hum beneath a tight band of perfectly punched words. "Maybe it's to protect you. Maybe it's the package, but if it's the latter—"

"Then he wants to disappear again and he can't do that if we're alive. I'm aware of how this plays out and that we won't know his true colors until we're at the end of this story, whatever this story truly is. But we also need the package. It's the ticket to ending all of this. And if we have to use each other—him us and us him—to find it, we have to do what we have to. We need this to just be over. *We need this over.*

"And if he wants us dead?"

"We make sure we kill him before he kills us."

# CHAPTER ELEVEN

## ANA

**TEN YEARS AGO...**

The cake says "Sweet Sixteen" and as I sit with a group of ten friends around the long table in their family dining room, I watch Lara Callahan's mother attempt to light the candles. When she fails, Lara's father rushes to the aid and finishes the job. He's a handsome guy, a banker, I heard from someone I think, and he waves his hands for everyone to applaud his efforts. We comply, of course, happily cheering, and while I am giddy with delight for Lara, there is this gnawing sensation in my belly that I cannot deny.

There are simply moments in life when I feel the loss of my mother and father more than others. I have Kurt, I do, and I'm thankful for that, but my sweet sixteen was me attempting to complete a drill to get to my cake.

Everything is about life or death, not just life.

Because he's the reason my mother was killed. He told me that himself. His enemies killed her. His enemies could come for me one day. The way they came for her.

It's hours later when I return to The Ranch and walk into the kitchen to find Kurt sitting at the table, drinking coffee, and working on his MacBook. My agitation at him is an abrupt punch that transforms into a choppy sensation of anger. I round the counter and grab a protein drink from the fridge, because God forbid I drink a soda. At least I had cake and ice cream tonight.

I shut the fridge door and he's standing there, big and intimidating as ever. "Please don't tell me I have to pay for the party with a four-mile run. I ran five this morning."

"Someone came home with attitude."

"Who killed my mother?"

His eyes narrow and his energy pops but his expression never changes. "We've had this conversation. My enemies."

"Who were the enemies?"

"They're dead, Ana. That's all you need to know."

"Then why are you still so afraid they'll come for me?"

"Not them. Someone else."

"Who?"

"There are bad people in this world."

"Are you one of them?"

His jaw tics. "Some people think I am."

"Are you?"

"Sometimes."

"Then why am I here?"

"Because you're my daughter."

"But I'm not really, am I?"

He stares at me for several beats, turns on his heels, and walks back to the table where he sits down. That gnawing sensation in my belly is back, but stronger now, with a sense of loss and guilt with it. Yes, he's my stepfather, and no we are not blood, but he didn't have to take me in or protect me. Without him, I'd be alone. And I do love Kurt.

I set the protein drink down and walk to the table, claiming the seat across from him. "I'm sorry."

"Don't be sorry," he states, tapping the table. "Do not ever be sorry for asking questions and excepting answers. It's your right."

"Who were they?" I demand.

"It's also my right not to answer. They're dead. That's all you need to know."

An image of Lara and her parents in front of that candle-lit cake flashes in my mind. I want to push him. I need to push him. But I've known Kurt most of my life. I know when he will bend. I know when he will not. And so, I say, "Goodnight."

"Goodnight," he replies, and I stand up, grab my protein drink, and walk toward the stairwell that leads downstairs where my bedroom is at.

Once I'm in my room, I shut the door, walk to the bed, drop to my knees and pull out my memory box. I lift the lid and pick up the photo of me and my mother when I was only a wee child. She was beautiful—blonde with striking eyes, and a smile that lit up the world. And in this photo, she was smiling at me. She loved me. And I loved her. But there is also another photo of her with Kurt, and she is smiling just as broadly at him as she had me, while he'd looked down at her with doe-eyed submission. Yes, submission. He would have done anything for her, even raised me and Kasey.

I try not to think about the obligation that might make me to Kurt.

Instead, I remind myself that he loved her to the moon.

He would never have intentionally put her in danger.

And yet, he did, more than put her in danger.

He got her killed.

**LISA RENEE JONES**

# CHAPTER TWELVE

## ANA

Once we're downstairs, inside the kitchen, Luke catches me to him and kisses me hard and fast but when he pulls back and stares down at me, his eyes say all that words do not dare with Kurt nearby. He's here. He understands how much this Kurt situation eats me alive, and God it does. It so does. And, of course, the real message Luke offers is that no matter how this shakes out, I'm not alone. I touch his cheek, my fingers dragging over the rough-edged stubble of his jawline, a "thank you" in that gentle connection. I know he's here. I know he's worried. That's all I need to know.

Forcing myself to leave him where he stands, I step backward and do so, despite an innate fear, no doubt created by this past two years, that any division between us will extend eternally. His hands fall away from my body, his eyes a storm of worry for me. Not physically I know, because Kurt is tied up, and I'm more than capable with my weapon of shooting him, and at this point, I won't hesitate to do so if necessary.

That doesn't mean I won't suffer afterward, but I will survive.

Kurt taught me to do no less.

I turn away from Luke and exit the kitchen.

Moments later, I bring the sitting area just outside the office into view to find Savage sitting in a chair across from Kurt, a gun on his lap. The two men are in a silent stare-off. God, I love Savage and I barely know him, but I know enough. He's just so damn Savage. The kind of man Kurt would respect. The kind of man Kurt will hesitate to test. Luke was one of those men to Kurt, but then I became Luke's weakness and I have no doubt Kurt will continue to use that against him.

I stand there and watch them watch each other, my mind drifting back to Lara's party. I'm sure had I been born her, I would have greeted my father with a hug and tears. But had I been Lara, my father would never have faked his death.

Closing the space between me and them, I motion for Savage to let me sit. He stands, his weapon in his hand, and steps to the rear of the chair, a protective stance to the way he plants his feet to stay a while. I motion at him again. "We need to be alone."

He arches a dark brown. "You sure about that?"

I'm warmed by his protectiveness, a sign that these brothers Luke has found in our time apart, welcome me with open arms. As Adam said, he would die for me. Savage would do the same, but I would not want to meet his wife in the aftermath. I want to meet her with him alive and well. That means I need Kurt to talk to me. Really talk to me.

I give a tiny nod. "Positive, but thank you, Savage."

He grunts. "I'm not positive," he rebuts, "but I'll be in the kitchen." He scowls at Kurt and then saunters in that direction.

I claim the seat in front of Kurt, and for a moment, just a moment, guilt stabs at me, for allowing the man who sheltered and cared for me, to sit tied to a chair. But then a memory surfaces, me in a cave, my hands, and feet tied up as punishment for being captured by the "enemy." The enemies were his men, and the mission was training at The Ranch. If my guilt was a word written on a chalkboard, my memories of his actions are the eraser that wipes it away, and does so in a clear, swift swipe.

"I knew you'd be back," he states, a gleam in his eyes that almost reads like pride, though this emotion is illogical for most, it's not for Kurt.

I tied him up. I took control. These are the actions of the person he taught me to become. More and more, I'm not sure I'm proud of that person. "Why come back now?"

"I told you why."

"Tell me again. Because based on what you've said thus far it's hard for me to believe you have a man on the inside of this operation we're battling. And yet, you got here. You knew we were coming and that indicates that you indeed, do have an insider view of what's going on."

"I hired a hacker, some guy out of Germany. He's monitoring everyone I know is involved, including Parker."

"Then you have to know who Parker was reporting to," I assume.

"Your boss, who's now dead. He emailed him. That's how they communicated. The three-day pledge was communicated to Mike."

"That means they also know we don't have the package."

"Parker wrote about his belief that you were coming here to The Ranch, because the package is hidden here. We still have three days."

I'm not sure I believe him, but I lean toward yes, at least on this. We all need to hope that's a fact. Right now, I want to know why he's back in this moment, and not a previous one. Aside from the idea that this package has surfaced.

"Were you working for or with Mike?" I ask, referencing my boss, who is now dead.

"No. A guy they called Maverick. Real name: Ted Maverick. He's dead."

"Did you kill him?"

He barks out a laugh. "I wish. I wanted to kill that little prick a hundred times over. He's the one who used you as a weapon against me. The only reason I let him live was because I wanted him to lead me to his boss. I wanted to end this. And he did. Or so I thought. That was your boss. Turns out he was Maverick's replacement. Once Mike came on the scene, Maverick had a heart attack. Translated to, he got himself killed off."

"When?"

"Right after Kasey died. You can see why Luke leaving right at that point in time, set about as well as spoiled milk sits with me. Real damn sour."

# CHAPTER THIRTEEN

## ANA

For just a moment, I'm back at Kasey's burial site, reliving that godforsaken, brutal day...

*I'm standing alone after everyone else has left, a cold drizzle tormenting my body, while the casket in front of me shreds my heart. Kasey is gone. Kurt is gone. And I don't even know what is happening with me and Luke. He killed Kasey, and damn him, I know Kasey was troubled, but why couldn't he have found a way to save him? Or let someone else do it at least. How am I supposed to love the man who killed my brother? Why do I still love him so damn much? And why isn't he here with me now?*

*It's then that I feel this tingling sensation, as if I'm being watched, and my gaze jerks up and toward a cluster of trees. Luke steps out of the coverage of those trees, and I'm both relieved and elated to see him here, well and alive, after the bullet that ended up in his gut. I didn't mean to shoot him, but some part of me knows, I should have wanted to shoot him. I was really trying to protect him from Trevor when my gun had fallen and I'd tried to catch it.*

*The next thing I knew I was trying to stop him from bleeding out.*

*It was a freak accident and had my emotions not gotten the best of me, it would never have happened.*

*But no matter how it happened, I shot him. I'll never make him believe it was an accident. He'll always hate me. And some part of me will hate him, too, for killing Kasey, even if I know Kasey forced his* hand. *The very fact that I haven't turned away from him now, that I am relieved to see him, stabs me with guilt. So much guilt.*

*I turn away from him and leave him standing there. I turn away from us, and it about kills me all over again.*

I blink back to the room and find Kurt watching me.

"Penny for your thoughts?"

*I forced Luke to leave*, I think, I drove him away, but I don't say this to Kurt. He doesn't want to hear my emotional confessions about me and Luke. All he's doing is distracting me from whatever he doesn't want me to figure out by triggering such thoughts and feelings. My lips press together and I dive into the deep, dark waters of the topic I think he's avoiding and I'm not sure why. "Why Maverick? Why kill him then?"

"Well, if you're reading this like I did, it feels a little like a threat, doesn't it? Almost as if they knew I was watching, but they didn't. I think your partner made them nervous."

There he goes distracting me again, but I punch back. "Darius wasn't my partner anymore."

"Close enough. You were with him often. He acted as a friend and a close confidant. That bond kept you both alive for a while. They thought he'd find out what you knew about the package. But he nosed around the wrong things and people, which would have been fine, but he got too confident. When you get too confident, you get sloppy. Even I could see that, and I wasn't up close and personal with him or you. But I *was* sure that your boss, Mike, being as high up in FBI as he was, was the train that led up the hill to the mighty king. I wanted the king."

"And you think that ends this?"

"It won't end these assholes, whoever they are, no. They're too big and their ties run too deep with the government and the rich and powerful. But maybe it ends the obsession with this particular package and our inner circle. It's hard to know. It's worth a try. That was my thought process, but that never happened. It feels like every time I get close, someone ends up dead."

Obviously, he means Maverick and Mike. "Who do you know that tells them you're close?"

"No one."

Now I know he's not being straight with me. "Wrong answer," I argue. "If there was no one to tell, there would be no one to share information with you."

"I told you. I hired a hacker. He's disconnected from the organization."

"Unless he isn't," I say. "Who's the buyer?" I ask, aware that the buyer is dead. We went to Newman Phillips' house, the man who was supposed to receive that package from Kasey, hoping to dig up at least a clue to follow. He was dead on our arrival.

"I don't know, but they're powerful enough to rattle the cages of the assholes when not much does. Normally if you get in their way, they kill you."

"Unless they have money to make, I assume," I reply, and yet they killed Newman Phillips, who per Darius's notebook was on the list of buyers. He was just rich, the son of the man who owns a professional sports team in Denver, and the man who was supposed to buy the package that went missing when Kasey died. "Why kill off your buyer?"

He arches a brow. "Are you telling me they did?"

"Why?" I press.

"Because you have another buyer. Or because the buyer has damning information. Or both."

"Are the men hunting us, and the package, working for the organization or the buyer?"

"I've heard both had treasure hunters working for them. And once one or the other finds the package, you're nothing but a liability that must be disposed of. You need to find that package."

*Says him and everyone else*, I think. I'm so tired of hearing about this damn package. "And do what with the package when we find it?" I ask, hoping he has some grand plan that actually makes sense.

"Give it to someone they fear. I have ideas on that, of course."

"Yes, fear is your favorite emotion," I say dryly, still admittedly bitter at his faked death and reappearance. "If you don't know who this organization is, how do you know what they fear?"

"You fight organized crime with organized crime. Pit them against each other, step back, and let them go to war and kill themselves off. But we have to find the package. The seller doesn't stop wanting it because one buyer is dead. He'll find another."

"We know we need the package. How do you suggest we find it?"

"The only chance we have of figuring that out is to become a buyer which just got easier if you're telling me they killed off the buyer to keep you from picking their brain. We need to attract the seller, convince them we have money, and intent to buy. That would be easier to do if we knew what was in the package. Bottom line, you need to trust me for me to help you."

"Just trust you?" I say and lean in closer. "You held a gun to my head, Kurt."

"You know I wasn't going to hurt you."

But that's the point, he doesn't understand. I knew Luke would never hurt me. I knew Luke would never have killed Kasey had he had any other option. Grief destroys people and relationships. You see it all the time. A couple loses a child and then they lose each other. I almost killed Luke. That thought has me flashing back to that day in the cemetery when Luke stepped out from behind the tree. I should have run to him. I should have held onto him. I will not lose him now because I too easily trust Kurt.

**LISA RENEE JONES**

# CHAPTER FOURTEEN

## ANA

I stare at Kurt, and I make sure he sees the contempt in my eyes. Because I feel contempt. I feel bitterness. I feel angry. "You say I knew you wouldn't hurt me?" I challenge. "I knew you were dead, too. I was wrong."

"Playing dead did the same thing holding that gun to your head did. It got the job done. Parker would have killed me to keep me from giving him up. In that moment, it was me or him. If I would have died then I wouldn't be telling you this now, would I? I kept my SIM card. It's buried in the old mine, next to Big Bear Rock. It'll verify a lot of what I told you about my activities and the threats against you before I disappeared. Get it. Go through it. Then you can untie me and we can get to work saving your life."

I sit back. "How do I know that's not a trap?"

"Why would I want to trap you out there?"

"To continue to manipulate Luke. You made him promise to protect me and now you're using that against him. That, in and of itself, tells you why I won't trust you."

"He left you, Ana. I had to know he was all in."

Unless it's more than that. Unless Kurt really is angry over Kasey's death. Unless all of this is some game Kurt is playing to get back at Luke. It's a farfetched idea, but my badge taught me never to rule out any theory before proving that theory wrong.

"*He left me?* That's why you're going after Luke? You really want me to believe that you have no bad feelings toward him because he killed Kasey?"

"I'm not going after Luke, Ana. But as I said, he left you. I simply wanted to get a clear picture of his motivations now that he's back by your side."

"By making him punch you."

"He's not a man that flies off the handle. He wouldn't have punched me if he didn't care about you."

"And that's it? That's all that worried you about Luke? There was no concern at all over him killing Kasey?"

"Kasey was begging for a grave. He was not a good man."

"You were—"

"His s*tepfather?*" he queries. "Yes, I was. And I get it. You think that because I'm not your blood, or his, that we're less connected. You're wrong. I loved your mother with all that I was and all that I am today. And I loved her kids, who became my kids. I chose to be your father. A biological father doesn't get to choose. I *chose* both of you. Kasey chose everyone else but us. Time is ticking, Ana. Go get that SIM card or send Savage. The man is named appropriately. He'll bring it back."

I consider him for a moment, and then, I don't agree or disagree with him. I simply stand up and walk toward the kitchen. My mind is racing with everything he's said to me. Darius dug around too much and I'm reminded about the key to a locker, or lockbox, he'd claimed to have left me. Maybe, just maybe he had a photo or information that meant nothing to him but everything to Kurt. Not that I trust Kurt, or plan to trust him ever.

But we're going to use him. We have no other option.

I round the corner to the kitchen and find Luke and Savage standing there. They're waiting on my assessment of Kurt but it's no different than it's ever been. Kurt is a man who gets what he wants, even if it's me running an obstacle course to earn my birthday cake, like living through sixteen years of death and tragedy wasn't enough to allow me one day to just eat cake. No matter what is on that SIM card, I'm going to struggle to believe he was forced into anything, including a grave. I'm also not ready to dismiss the idea that we don't really know what is going on, and Kurt has set us up, or rather Luke, by way of an elaborate show.

He loves to make a mockery of people. The very thought tells me that I'm going to struggle to trust him. And the minute my eyes meet Luke's, I see the same doubt in his eyes.

We're in agreement. Trusting Kurt is not an option. The problem is, there's more in Luke's eyes than just distrust for Kurt. He heard all of the questions I asked Kurt about holding Kasey's murder against him. He thinks I went there because I can't let go of the fact that he killed Kasey, so logically, in his eyes, I thought Kurt couldn't either. And he's wrong. Which I'll tell him but not now. We can't deal with that now. The clock is ticking on our three days to find the package. We have to conquer our enemies before they conquer us.

**LISA RENEE JONES**

# CHAPTER FIFTEEN

## LUKE

I killed Kasey.

That Ana thinks all of this, every last freaking nightmare moment of it, is about Kurt claiming revenge against me, it undoes me. Kurt was "dead" before I ever killed Kasey but that's not where her head is at right now. The bottom line here is that Kasey is still standing firmly between us, even from the other side.

But I let it go for now and so does she, as Savage keeps us both focused on the immediate need for action. "I can go retrieve the SIM card," he offers.

Ana rejects that idea with a wave of her hand. "I really don't care what's on that SIM card. He's a master of deception. Anything on that card could all be fake. And he's gotten out of worse circumstances than a chair and ropes when he wasn't watched. Please just make sure he doesn't go anywhere."

"I can drug him," Savage offers, as nonchalant as if he offered to bring him coffee. "He'll snooze, maybe snore a little, drool all unmanly like but I can wake him back up if you make me."

Ana arches a brow. "If I make you?"

"I sure as fuck won't wake him up by choice," he assures her.

*Smart man*, I think. Ana hesitates and then says, "He's dangerous. Maybe you should."

"Right-e-o. Good decision," Savage approves. "A nap it is, and then me and the Big Bear Rock have a date. I'll go after the SIM card. Blake will know what's real and what's not." He disappears into the living room.

Ana motions to the garage and starts walking. I hesitate, replaying that conversation she had with Kurt in my head. *You really want me to believe that you have no bad feelings toward him because he killed Kasey?*

The memory grinds through me, driving home the fact that I'm living in a dream world with Ana, but damn it, not even this makes me want to stop. I'm all about living the pipe dream apparently. I scrub my jaw and rotate on my heels, following Ana to the garage. At this point, Ana's already climbing into the SUV we rode to The Ranch in, which one of the guys moved into the garage. I follow her inside and find her on the opposite side of the backseat, digging in the bag where we stored everything we retrieved from Darius's cabin.

By the time I've shut us inside, she's holding the tape recorder. "Darius said there was a key in here to a locker or lockbox. I don't remember which. We just dismissed it, focused on what was in hand."

"Lockbox. And we didn't forget. We just got swept into torrential, bloody waters. Everyone around us keeps dropping dead before we get to them."

"But we came here to stand our ground after we found out Mike and Newman were dead. What about Newman's father, the real billionaire? We should be talking to him, looking for the lockbox, and finding the package. Being we're *here* doing nothing." She's not done yet. She's fired up obviously as she adds, "The package isn't here. Maybe the lockbox is the key to finding the package. Maybe there's a picture in there of someone Kurt will know."

I arch a brow. "Do you trust Kurt to tell us if he does?"

"No, but he's all we have."

"Darius has more to offer that I actually trust more than Kurt. Where's the lockbox?"

"I don't know," she says, frustration etched in her words. "We didn't even find a key. Did we?"

"Not that I saw."

"Darius said on the recording that it was in the stuff we found at the cabin. And he said it like I should know where the lockbox is. Did we drop the key? And why did we not realize we missed this?"

"Like I said, we've had our hands full." I grab the bag she's holding and start digging around.

"I want to listen to the audio again," she says, and still holding the recorder, she fast-forwards and hits play, somehow managing to land on just the right spot:

*I'm not going to get into the when, why, and how bullshit,* Darius says, *inside the notebook, you'll find a list of packages that I know were delivered, with dates, and buyers' names. I don't know what was in the packages. I didn't want to know. I wasn't even involved in that side of things, but you know how I roll. I wanted to know what I was involved with. I did some digging. I followed someone important to the operation. I recorded his conversations. I took photos. There's a key in the bag. It goes to a lockbox loaded with that shit.*

*On to the topic of Kasey...Yes, let that sink in a moment—on to the topic of Kasey.*

*You'll find the one Kasey was delivering highlighted. The buyer won't know who the big boss was, because there was a frontman. That would be our boss, Ana. Mike is the one who pulled me into this.* He laughs. *See, I said I wasn't going to talk about the when, where, and how or any of that bullshit, but turns out I have to in order to get you this information.*

Ana turns off the recording. "It's like he jumped from the lockbox, back to talking about the notebook, where he listed the deliveries out. He forgot to tell us where the lockbox is located. I swear if he wasn't dead, I'd kill him right now."

I start patting down the exterior of the bag, and bingo, I find a bulge that feels like a key. With the help of my trusty pocket knife, I cut the key out of the bag and hold it up. "The sticker on the side reads *The River Box 21*. Does this mean anything to you?" I hand the key to Ana.

She glances at it and murmurs, "He didn't forget to tell us where the lockbox is located." She holds the key up. "The River is code for a gym in downtown Denver he went to during an undercover operation. They have a hot tub he called a river because it was always so dirty. I guess he didn't forget. We have to go there. Now, Luke."

"All right. Let's go." I reach for the door.

She scoots closer and grabs my arm. "Whatever you think you heard—"

Anger comes at me with surprising depth. "He's not here for me, Ana. And clearly, you aren't either."

"That's not true. Why do we keep going there?"

"I didn't go there. I don't go there, Ana. You do."

"No," she insists. "I do not. You keep assuming—"

"*Assuming*?" I demand. "I heard what you said to him. Why wouldn't he hate me if I killed his son?"

"Why wouldn't he? For you to think that's not an option is denial Luke. If he loved Kasey, he would have had some kind of animosity toward you. We need to know it's not at play."

"Because you have animosity toward me?"

"Me being confused over you back then was natural in the aftermath of a loss. It was shock and grief that

I've had two years to deal with and regret. He hasn't seen you since it happened. If he can truly tune that out, he's cold. He's callous."

"He's Kurt, Ana. Of course, he's cold and callous. That doesn't mean he didn't care about Kasey. I cared about Kasey. I wanted him to turn it around but he didn't have that in him. You're the one with the referendum on Kasey that says everyone should fight for him when he fought for no one but himself."

She swallows hard. "I know. He's Kurt. Maybe I just—you know, if he doesn't fight for Kasey, why would he fight for me?"

"He answered that for you ten different ways," I remind her, I also remind myself that I hungered for a family after losing my parents at a young age. She's clinging to the one man she knew as a parent and craving a reaction from him that makes him worthy of that title. "I know you want something from him he's not giving you, baby."

"No," she says adamantly. "No. I'm worried about you as a target."

"His best friend is dead, Ana. If this was about me, Jake wouldn't be dead." I stroke her hair back from her face. "You are not thinking logically where Kurt is concerned, and whether you realize it or not, that's because he hurt you."

"He trained the emotion out of me, Luke. You know that."

"You are not Kasey. He didn't train it out of you. I think I've proven that just by existing in your life. And that's a good thing, Ana. It's why you wear that badge with compassion, honesty, and strength, the way it's supposed to be worn."

Her fingers bunch around my shirt. "You're right. I'm emotional, over you. His presence feels like a knife about to cut you from my life. Why can't you see my questioning as that? As my need to protect you, not my need to blame you."

Guilt stabs at me over my reaction. She's right. I need to stop cornering her reactions with a label that reads as the blame game against me. I lean in, my lips close to hers, my breath hot on her cheek when there's a knock on the window. I curse and kiss her hard and fast. "I will do better," I vow, and already there's another knock only this time more insistent.

It's a reminder that we can make all the promises to each other in the world, but until this is over, we have no time, or way, of acting on those promises. Nothing matters until this is over. And damn it to hell, if I need to go kill some people to make that happen, let Lucifer come out to play.

It's time to do some damage to our enemies.

# CHAPTER SIXTEEN

## LUKE

I get out of the SUV to find Adam and Savage standing at the front of the garage. Obviously, Kurt's now sleeping. Ana slides out beside me and I shut the door. "What now?" I ask.

"Blake cleared the house," Adam replies. "Satellite shows no movement."

"There are places people can hide and go unseen," Ana replies, "but I still don't believe Kurt would allow himself to be tied up if we were going to be attacked."

"He didn't allow shit," Savage replies. "We overtook him."

"Maybe," I say. "Maybe not. Either way, we need to get off this ranch while anyone who might be here is tucked away."

"What do we know about Maverick or Phillips Senior?"

"Nothing that helps," Adam replies. "These people know how to stay off the radar."

"Of course," I say, feeling fed up with getting nowhere. "Phillips Senior would be our obvious next stop."

"As obvious as the big ass nose on that man's face. Believe me, I saw his picture. Too damn obvious."

"He's right," Adam replies. "They'll be waiting for us. Blake will continue to use our resources to connect them in any way he can to the package. Blake also sent us help and that help is here and active. Dexter, Wyatt, and Smith. Smith and Wyatt are watching Phillips Senior. Dexter is watching for the next name on that list in Darius's notebook. Right now, that's led us nowhere."

"Darius left us a key to a lockbox we've now located," Ana replies. "Maybe something inside that box will connect the dots we need connected."

"Where is it?" Adam asks.

"A gym in downtown Denver," Ana replies.

"If that box is on the wrong radar," Adam replies, "it could be a trap. We need to pull one of the guys and have them help. Smith is my suggestion."

"Agreed," I say. "I'll text him and meet up with him."

"I need to go get that SIM card before we leave," Savage replies. "There might be something on there Blake can use."

"That's time we don't have," I reply. "That could trigger anyone hiding out to come out to play."

"And yet we need that SIM card," Adam chimes in. "I agree with Savage. We need to divide and conquer. We'll stay here with Kurt and work him as a source. You two go to the lockbox with Smith."

Ana eyes me and gives a small nod.

"All right then," I say, "then that's the plan," because what else can I say? I can't even figure out who to go punish right now to make this right. The only way to change that is to find something that tells me who deserves my wrath, and I've got plenty to go around.

And right now, we have a whole lot of nothing going on while the clock ticks on our three remaining days which are now two and some hours.

"Well, then let me get to it," Savage says, his stare fixed on Ana. "Where's the fucking Big Bear Rock, sweet pea? And where are all the booby traps your pop set-up? I'd rather not get blown up today. My birthday is in a month. My wife never refuses back rubs during my birthday month."

"I need paper and a pen," Ana says, and when Adam produces them, she writes out a whole hell of a lot of notes.

Savage eyes it all and grunts. "Well, it was a good life when I was here." He glances around the group. "Tell my wife I loved her. Holy hell there's a shit ton of booby traps."

"Just follow the cross," Ana says, showing him the way the clear path represents a cross. "And yes, that was on purpose. Kurt said anyone who survives that path has God on his side."

"Fuck Kurt," Savage grumbles. "I'll be back in ten minutes, but I reserve the right to punch Kurt for putting me through that, even if you decide you trust him, Ana."

"Please do," Ana says. "He deserves it."

I motion to her toward the SUV and start walking.

Once we're both sealed inside, the keys are in the ignition, and I start the engine. Adam hits the button by the door to open the garage. Once we're driving toward the gates of The Ranch, a sense of relief washes over me. The Ranch is a death sentence, at least for me and Ana. I don't care if we never come back.

**LISA RENEE JONES**

# CHAPTER SEVENTEEN

## LUKE

We clear the gates of The Ranch without any trouble. And yet trouble has her sights on us and with such determination, we might as well be riding downhill with an overloaded eighteen-wheeler roughing up our bumper.

On that note, I'm fairly confident anyplace we go, and anything we can do could be a trap. Apparently, I'm not the only one thinking the same. My earbuds start to read a text in my ears: *Message from Blake: I'm reviewing the camera feed for the gym, the hotel next to it, and the street around both. More soon.*

We're about five miles down the highway, headed toward town when Ana glances over at me. "I can't believe he's alive." She glances over at me. "I can't believe he's alive, Luke."

This, right now, I realize, is really the first quiet time she's had to step back and take in the reality of the situation. "I can't believe he's alive either, baby."

"And we drugged him," she says. "Proof of how abnormal my life truly is. I shot you and drugged him."

"The gun had a faulty discharge and Savage drugged him, but if he's the man we both once knew, he'd approve of your warrior spirit. And as for normal, it doesn't exist."

"You had a normal childhood, Luke, and I swear that's why you survived what you have with a level head on your shoulders,"

"My father died during active duty. My mother died a week before I enlisted. I guess it depends on how you define normal."

"They were in love and happy."

"If that was all it took to be normal, we'd be normal, Ana, and we're not. But yes, my parents were in love. And the two of them together and happy, represent good memories for me that often get overshadowed by me losing them back-to-back, one year to the next." As sure as I say those words, my mind is traveling back home, to a Christmas morning, with me, my mom, and dad around the tree. The next I know though, I'm remembering the day I left that all behind, and boarded a plane to leave for flight school, without my father around to see me do it. God, that still hurts. The only thing that hurt as much as losing my parents was losing Ana.

"I wish I would have met them, Luke."

"I wish you would have, too, baby," I say, shaking off the memories and refocusing on the here and now. "Kurt loved your mother. He spoke about her to me often,"

"We think," she counters. "I don't know, I barely remember them together. I was so young when they married, and she was gone not long after."

I motion to the highway that is backed up with standstill traffic. "We won't be going that way."

"Wonderful," she says. "Can we not just find answers and be done with this?" She shivers and reaches for her coat in the backseat, pulling it over her, and then cutting a sharp look in my direction. "You know, I just realized we never took our coats inside and The Ranch was warm. I keep the heat way down. Kurt had been at the house a while. Could he really have been living there?"

"I doubt he's been living there the whole three years but the idea that he's been using it, even off and on that entire time, doesn't really shock me. He's way more involved in this mess than we are, and we're completely consumed."

"And I never knew," she murmurs.

"I wish I could give you answers, Ana. I wish I could turn back time and make everything wrong, right, but the problem with that premise is that we were never in control. At least not then."

"You think we're in control now?"

"These assholes are so desperate to find this package that they're counting on us to deliver it, and we don't even know what's inside. When we're the resource that allows them to get what they want, yes, we have control. Unless someone finds the package before we do. Then we become disposable." I turn us off the access road and begin the winding path toward downtown.

"Why are they this desperate now?" she asks, almost talking to herself before her voice lifts and she repeats, "Why *now?* I keep going back to that in my mind. Why now? Why go after Jake? Why use him to lure us together? And if Newman was their buyer, why kill him off when the package has surfaced and could be potentially sold for what is obviously a big payday?"

"Maybe someone really tried to sell the package. Or maybe there's another buyer with a bigger payday which brought this front and center again."

"Maybe they didn't kill off the buyer. Maybe, it was always Phillips Senior who was the buyer."

"Killing off his son isn't exactly the way to win him over," I remind her.

"Kurt said he heard the buyer hired his own team to find the package. What if Newman was trying to push out the middleman? Maybe it's even Phillips Senior trying to push out the middleman, meaning the organization, so they killed his son?"

"I'd buy that as a big possibility, but right when we went to see him? That's a big coincidence."

"But possible."

"I'm skeptical about the timing."

"Turn them against each other," she murmurs, under her breath, and then says, "Kurt suggested we create an enemy for our enemy, someone to take the attention off of us. God. Did he kill Newman to turn Phillips Senior against the organization?"

"If he did, he kept him from talking which doesn't sit right. It reads like he's working for them. And in support of that theory, if this operation is as big as he says they are, one rich dude who owns a sports team would not be enough to distract them."

"The idea that he's working for them is not a good one, but one we keep coming back to and I don't like how easily that happens. It means it feels right to us both. But as you say, it is what it is. If Phillips got shut out for another buyer, maybe he'll be willing to talk. Or maybe he'll want to help us catch his son's killer."

"Or he'll blame us for his son's murder and come at us, and we have two enemies. I'm all for going right at the bull, but we need more facts. Maybe between Kurt and Darius, today is the day we make that happen."

My cellphone rings and I glance down to find Savage calling. "Savage," I say. "That was fast." I punch answer on the Caller ID. "Savage. You're on speaker."

"I've got the SIM card. Adam's uploading it for Blake to review." He yawns. "A little too easy a ride out there, Ana. Your old man isn't all he's cut out to be."

My lips curve and I glance at Ana. "That's the junior range, Savage," she teases. "The one for the slow learners. That's why I knew you'd be just fine."

"Hey hey hey now," he complains. "I don't like your tone. Your pop is going to wake up soon. I'll feed him and then make him talk. I mean we'll chat. It will be fun. Ciao." He hangs up.

"Don't worry," I say. "He won't hurt him. He'll drive him so fucking nuts he can't help but talk."

Ana laughs one of her soft, sweet laughs, but there's a choked quality to her voice.

"He's not going to hurt him, baby. And in my gut, I believe Kurt really means to do right by you. He's not going to disappear again."

She gives a choppy nod. But she says nothing. What is there to say?

Everything that was real is now a lie.

The truth is either going to save us or kill us once and for all. And right now, the closest thing to the truth we have to look forward to is in a lockbox that a dirty cop, who was spying on Ana, left us.

**LISA RENEE JONES**

# CHAPTER EIGHTEEN

## LUKE

We pull into a parking spot at the McDonald's where we're supposed to meet Smith when my cellphone rings with Smith's number. "Yeah, man, we're here," I answer. "Where are you?"

"Stuck in traffic hell. I'm not getting there anytime soon. You might as well have a burger, or ten, while you wait for me." I grimace and glance at Ana.

"He's caught in that traffic we avoided."

Ana's head drops and then she says, "We're on a timer. We need to do this."

"Agreed," I say and then return to Smith. "I'll let you know if we need you. Call me when you get out of traffic." I disconnect. "Texting Blake," I tell Ana, before I shoot off the message that reads: *We need anything you have for us now. We're headed over to the club. Smith is caught in traffic.*

I hit send and refocus on Ana. "I told Blake we need whatever he can get us. It's just you and me, baby. We're going to have to make it work."

"I doubt anyone is watching Darius's locker anyway," she says. "They didn't know about his cabin. They won't know about this."

"We don't know how long ago he left that stuff at the cabin. Don't be so sure he wasn't being watched on a day-to-day basis and we have no idea how many times he went to this locker and added information. It could be exactly how he got busted and ended up dead."

My cell rings with Blake's number and I answer on speaker. "You have me and Ana, Blake."

"I heard about Smith's delay. There's a hotel attached to the fitness club. I booked you a room. I would suggest Ana stay in the room when you go to the locker, Luke. Ana, I know you're going to object, but these people are going to use you against Luke where they can. They proved that by using you as bait to get him to Colorado. Not to mention the two of you together are more obvious."

"I'm worried about someone having his back," Ana replies. "Do we have cameras to rely on anywhere near the locker?"

"We do not," Blake replies. "The club has limited cameras for privacy reasons but you can't back him up anyway. The men's locker room is on the opposite side of the gym from the women's."

"But is there equipment by the door? I can at least watch the door."

"It's a long hallway," he states. "I'm sending you the floor plan, and membership cards to the gym. You have reservations under your fake name, Luke. You have that ID, right?"

"I have it," I reply.

"Good. You'll need it at the hotel. There's a parking garage for the hotel. It's less obvious than the street or valet. It has cameras. I'll have eyes on you. Stay on the first level. There are open spots."

"Got it," I reply. "What else?"

"I suggest you check into the room, look over the floorplan for the gym, and leave Ana in the room. It's all coming at you now. There is one problem I need to bring up and it's a big one. I found Darius on the camera feed the night before he died. He knew he had heat on him because that was after your attack, Ana, and he still went to that locker. Don't count on that locker being anything but empty. When you're done there, and back in the room, I'll clear your exit path and we'll talk about my research. And no, nothing you need to know now. Get this done. Anything I know might come together with information in that locker." He disconnects.

I shift us into reverse. "I'll argue my points on me not staying in the hotel room while you drive," Ana says. "I can't see anyone targeting you if I'm in a room."

I pull us to the end of the driveway and onto the road, which is actually the road where the club is located. "I'll argue my side of this once we park or you'll win this battle and I'm not going to let that happen."

"We'll see," she retorts, but she doesn't press. Both of us have our eyes on the street, on our surroundings and it's not long before I pull us into the garage. Once I've backed us into a spot against the wall, that allows rapid exit, I kill the engine and turn to Ana. "They won't kill me, Ana. They want the package. They see us both as the ticket to get it. But they might do as Blake suggested and use you against me. Also, as Blake said, they've proven they're willing to do that and more."

"I do not like everyone using me as a weapon against you."

"If you're talking about Kurt, I don't think it's that simple. And you can call yourself a weakness, but I call you a reason to live. Which is why I need you to stay in the hotel room."

"It works in reverse. They could use you against me. They used Darius because they felt I had the package."

"It's the men's locker room, Ana. Let me have peace to know you're safe. That's going to allow me to get in and out fast, and without distraction."

Worry and reluctance dance across her beautiful face, but she concedes. "Fine. But I'm giving you a time limit or I'm coming after you. What's the plan to get into the hotel?"

Our phones buzz with a text message and I glance down to find the expected—an electronic key to a room Blake managed to make ours. "We have a room. We have an electronic key, thanks to Blake. We're going to the first floor for easy exit."

"It's also more visible," Ana says. "Less chance of someone coming at us there."

"Exactly. Unless you object, we'll go there first and make sure Blake has us on camera."

"That works," she says and slides on her coat. "You should take the backpack we have with us. It looks legit like you're headed into the locker room to change for your workout and you can put what you find inside it."

"You read my mind," I say, indicating my phone. "Blake sent us a roadmap to the two buildings."

She nods and we both study the layout, the direction we're traveling to our room, and to the club. I give us both one full minute and then reach for my door. Ana does the same for hers.

Once I'm outside I open the rear door and pull on my coat, simply to look more legit, and because it hides the extra gun I pull from under the seat and stick it in my belt at my back. Next, I grab the backpack and meet Ana at the front of the car.

At this point, we're out in the open and neither of us is focused on anything but our surroundings. The garage appears empty and we start walking. We're inside an elevator quickly, and I punch the lobby level. Kurt once told me a story of watching a friend get shot the fuck up the minute the elevator doors opened on him. Years later, I saw it happen to someone else. Ana must know that story because, in unison, both of us step to one side of the car, away from the door. That's where we stay until the doors are open, and we determine it's safe to exit.

Once we're in the lobby, a few people mill about but no one raises a red flag. Ana and I find the room signs and follow the arrow to our destination. Once we're at the door to our room, I use our electronic key and we're inside. She enters first, and by the time I'm inside, she's already searching the room. When we're all clear, she tosses her coat on the bed and lays down her rules. "The club is basement level and through a door," she says. "It should take you five minutes to get to the locker. Another three to unlock it and pack it up. Another five to return to this room. You have twelve minutes, from the time you leave me here to return, or I'm coming after you. And that's too long as far as I'm concerned," she states.

"That adds up to thirteen minutes."

"Not if you go faster. Go faster, Luke."

I laugh at her demand, and she scowls in reaction. "This isn't funny," she reprimands. "Do you know how intense it will be for me to wait here and worry about you?"

I toss my backpack on the bed, catch her to me, and stroke her hair from her face. "When I told you I had a reason to live, I meant it. I missed the hell out of you, woman. I'll be back." I kiss her, and not fast or gently. I close my mouth over hers, tongue stroking deep, drinking her in, every last drop of sweet, sexy woman, I can dare right now, in this room with danger punching at our door. It's with a herculean effort that I tear my mouth from hers and promise, "Eleven minutes." I release her, grab my bag, walk to the door, and fuck me, leaving her in that room feels as if I'm leaving her forever.

As I walk away, I decide eleven minutes just became ten.

# CHAPTER NINETEEN

## LUKE

My walk to the fitness club is eventless.

I'm at the club check-in desk, scanning my electronic entry pass, also compliments of Blake, in about three of the ten minutes I've given myself. I'm questioning the sanity of that timeline vow right about now but still determined to see it through. Ana will come after me and I need her in that room and protected.

I'll make the damn ten-minute mark.

Once I'm on the other side of check-in, I evaluate the workout area and size up any potential threat. I find everyone in my view either eyeing how they look in the mirrors lining the walls, focused on chatting it up with a friend, or sweating up a storm. No one sets off alarms.

The locker room sign directs me to my right, on the other side of the leg equipment, and as it turns out, down a set of stairs. Once I'm inside that private room, I find a bunch of sinks, a shower room, and then several cubby-like rooms with benches surrounded by lockers.

As for people, there are none outside of a couple of guys in the showers talking it up like a couple of naked fools. I mean holy hell—what makes a man stand next to another man naked and think it's time to talk about the Broncos football season, specifically their ball-handling skills?

*Get me the fuck out of here*, I think, eyeing the numbers on the first cubby of lockers and moving onto cubby number two. Once I'm there, this mission ends quickly. Darius's locker is wide open and empty. It's clear to see there's also no lock. Damn it to hell. Please, Lord, tell me he wrote the number down wrong. It's a long shot, but I have to try to find a better answer than I have at present. I survey the rest of the lockers, looking for a similar number, and actually try the key in the locks.

Some big-bellied dude, in a barely-there towel, rounds the corner and huffs out a protest. "Hey, man, that's my locker."

"Sorry, man. I could have sworn it was mine." I scrub my jaw. "My bad." I leave him standing there in his itty bitty towel and I can't do it fast enough.

Darius taught us all a lesson about pushing our luck. Not with a dude in a barely-there towel in the locker room, and definitely not with our enemies.

# CHAPTER TWENTY

## ANA

*Where you start doesn't define where you end.*
The man who recruited me into the FBI told me that.

I pace the small hotel room, waiting on Luke, counting down the minutes with those wise words in my head. Luke and I started out amazing. The end is not always the end. We are not over unless, of course, we end six feet under. The very idea that this is even a possibility in my mind, has me asking myself how we got here? How did two such trained individuals become prisoners to someone else's rule? And a stranger at that.

Yet, we have.

Collapsing onto the bed, I'm not defeated, but problem-solving, thinking back to the beginning, or trying to figure out where the beginning of all of this really even started. When I was eighteen, I graduated college, and I did so knowing the FBI was in my future. It was the iron fist of law enforcement to me, protectors that were not corruptible. Of course, I was young and naïve, as all human beings are corruptible. In some people's books, I might be considered a fool for ever believing such things, but in my defense, they'd started their recruitment efforts when I was about fifteen. It all started with George, one of the highest-ranking members of the agency who ever spent time at The Ranch.

George had been a teddy bear and a warrior, which would only make sense to those who knew George. He's gregarious and warm, but somehow no less lethal for it. He praised me as I worked out with him and his team, and later sat by the fire with me, and ate s'mores while telling me his old war stories, as he recalled his past with the FBI. He reminded me of my father, or at least the man, the child I was when I lost him, remembered. Or maybe George gave me a way to remember him.

He wasn't like George, the FBI agent, at all.

My father was a soldier, but even as my mother told it, a gentle man who took orders and stood for his country.

George became a perfect cross between Kurt and my father, the man I'd secretly wished was my father, and alternatively felt anguish and guilt for that betrayal of Kurt.

Maybe I deserve his betrayal now.

He knew he *knows,* that George personally recruited me and pushed hard to ensure I became one of them. I used to be proud of that fact. Now I'm thinking about who I need to kill inside the agency to stay alive. I can't think further enough into the future to contemplate what that means for me when this is over.

The door opens and instinct kicks in. I'm on my feet, gun in my hand, and aimed at the door, even as Luke appears. The sight of him, knowing he's alive and well, is exactly what I need right now. I breathe out and I swear the relief I feel permeates every pore in my body. I set the gun down on the dresser and hurry toward him, even as he flips the lock into place.

"Well?" I press, praying for an answer that will allow us all to survive this and start over.

He drops his backpack on the floor, his handsome face grim, a short shake of his head before he says, "Nothing. Cleaned out. I even talked to the front desk.

No luck. I think it's safe to assume that there was evidence against your boss in that locker, that made him a liability. Maybe on Newman, too, which would explain why he was dead when we got to him."

I press my hand to my head and then drop it. "I don't even know what to say anymore. We have what might as well be two days now until we meet up with these people and we have nothing. Not one little answer."

"The people we're meeting are hired hands, not the real boss. We just need to bypass them and go to that person."

"No one knows who he is, Luke," I remind him.

"Someone knows," he insists. "Probably Kurt."

"He doesn't know. I don't even know. He's trying to get answers from us, not the other way around. That's my take." I shake my head. "I can't believe I'm saying this but maybe it's time we disappear until we figure this out."

"No," Luke says. "Once you run, you're always running. Look at Kurt."

"Isn't that what we're doing anyway?" I challenge. "Running? We need to disappear until we can figure out what comes next."

His hands come down on my arms and he drags me to him. "No more waiting Ana."

"It's not waiting. It's planning."

"That's all I did when we were together before. I planned. I wanted to buy you a ranch and horses, therefore I kept taking jobs. I wouldn't have been overseas if I wouldn't have kept saying to wait to retire. Just one more job. No more waiting, Ana."

"It's not the same thing," I argue. "We're not waiting. We're planning."

"I'm over planning, Ana. I've already decided how we handle this. I'm going to kill whoever I need to kill, and I won't stop until everyone who can hurt you is dead."

"Luke—"

"Ana," he says, his mouth lowering to mine. "You know what I want right now?"

"Apparently to kill people."

"I do, but not as much as I want us both naked right now. I need to be inside you. I need to be fucking you. I need you wanting me to fuck you."

I laugh in disbelief. "We're not safe here."

"We're safe enough. Blake has eyes on the cameras. I have eyes on you. We're living in the moment, baby. Right here. Right now, because there might not be another."

"That's why we need to run, to regroup—"

He kisses me, a deep, drugging slide of his tongue, and before I even know what's happened, I'm against the wall, his strong body framing mine, overwhelming me in a good, but oh so poorly timed way. I moan with the taste of him, fighting to stay mentally aware of where we are and the dangers of the "moment" as he calls this.

"No running," he declares, stroking the hair from my face. "No more running."

"Luke—"

"Ana."

"Stop doing that," I chide, which isn't easy when he's touching me. This man and his hands have always been my undoing.

He catches the hem of my shirt. I catch his hand. "We're exposed here."

"If they kill me with you naked and in my arms, I'll die a happy man. It's this or I go kill people now, Ana. It's your call."

His mouth closes down on mine again, and somehow, I lose my sanity enough that my shirt ends up over my head, but I don't fight him. An action that's a product of a realization. He just said all he needs to say. Luke really does want to go kill everyone right now. Because there's a side of Luke most people don't know, a wild side that both turns me on and terrifies me. He's there now, on edge, and in a big way. If he doesn't come down and come down fast, then it's going to get bloodier than it has to. Or maybe bloodier sooner than it has to.

Either way, he's not wrong.
If this is how we die, this is how we die.

**LISA RENEE JONES**

# CHAPTER TWENTY-ONE

## LUKE

When I'd walked out of that locker room, I'd been coming out of my own skin. These people have torn our lives apart. They're the reason I killed Kasey. They're the reason I lost Ana and myself in the process. And I still don't even know who they are. But when I find out, and I will, they're dead.

Control.

I don't like not having it. I won't let us ride this problem out without finding it again.

For now, I'll settle for Ana on my cock, riding me, and doing it now. I run my hand down her back and unhook her bra, sliding it over her shoulders, and pressing her arms to the wall over her head. My gaze rakes over her breasts. My cellphone rings and my teeth grind. Damn it to hell, not now. I grab my phone, eye Blake's number on caller ID, and force myself to answer, before shoving it back in my pocket and speaking to him on my earbuds. "Yeah."

"You gonna update me?"

"It was empty." But I'm not right now. Not with Ana leaning on that wall, with her naked breasts right in my face.

I tease her nipples and she catches my hands as if Blake can see what we're doing.

"Fuck," he replies.

*Fuck is right*, I think. *Just let me off this phone to fuck my woman.*

"Where's your head at?" he asks.

"I need a minute to think."

"Agreed. Stay put. Let me think through our options. I'll call you in fifteen or sooner if you need to evacuate."

"Copy that, boss." I hit the button on my earbuds and disconnect.

"He wants us to lay low. He'll call if there's a problem. Long story short, we have minutes to fuck our brains out. Any objections?" I run my index finger around her nipples.

She catches my hands. "No."

I arch a brow.

"Then why are you holding onto my hands?"

"Because you keep teasing me."

"You know it, baby," I say, turning her to face the wall, and forcing her to catch herself on the hard surface. It's a submissive position and for a good reason. As much as I like it when Ana is fierce and demanding, there are times when I like her to submit. And she likes it, too. It was a realization that set our relationship on fire. I'd had a bad day, a fucked-up day. I actually lost a man on a job overseas. It was a freak accident. He'd been leaning out of the chopper, trying to get a ground view, and he'd caught his jacket on the door, slipping as he did. One of the other men all but went over with him trying to save him.

I'd come home a mess, but Ana had been at work. I'd gone straight to the bar and poured a drink, desperate to kill the pain of that loss. Ned had been the man's name. He had two fucking kids. I'd been on the couch, in the dark, halfway through a bottle when Ana had arrived. She'd known something was wrong, obviously.

*She goes down on her knees in front of me, her hands on my body, a lightning rod of adrenaline. I need to fuck and I'm hard and ready.*

*"Talk to me," she encourages.*

*"I don't want to talk, baby," I confess honestly. "That's not what I need right now."*

*Her eyes widen. "That bad?"*

*"That bad," I confirm.*

*"Then I'm here. Tell me what you need."*

*"I need you to stand up and undress, and that's just the beginning."*

*Understanding dawns in her eyes, deep in those intelligent eyes but there's no fear or hesitation. She uses my legs to push off the floor and stand up. She undresses then, and truly I don't know who is more in control right now. I am that lost in just watching her. When she's naked, she just stands there in front of me, as if she's waiting on instructions. And I give them to her.*

*"Turn around," I order.*

She turned around and damn the things I did to her that night.

We didn't speak about Ned until morning.

And now here she is again, her hands in front of her and me behind her.

**LISA RENEE JONES**

# CHAPTER TWENTY-TWO

## LUKE

### "DON'T LET YESTERDAY USE UP TOO MUCH OF TODAY."

### —WILL ROGERS

You'd think with Ana naked and at my mercy, I wouldn't be thinking about anything but fucking her. But fuck me, for just the briefest of moments, I'm living all the hell we've been through all over again. That confrontation with Kasey. The fight with Ana when I returned. The hospital. The funeral. That phone call from Jake when he was murdered as I listened. And then his warning about Ana, and my fear that our enemies would get to her before I did. And then that damn empty locker that tells me I'm no closer to ending all of this than I was two years ago.

All of it leads to right here and now, and how damn badly I need her and this escape.

But I'm not in a rush, even if our circumstances demand otherwise.

No.

I will not rush any moment I have with Ana. Not ever again.

I step into her, my hips pressed to her hips, my hands sliding up to cup her breasts, the puckered pebbles of her nipples against my palms, my lips pressing to her bare shoulder, teeth scraping the delicate skin there. She moans one of her sweet little moans and presses into me. Confirmation that she's let go of the world outside. She's present with me all the way, and that's exactly what I was looking for in her.

I reach for her pants, working them free until my hands are pressed beneath the material and I'm sliding them over her hips. I yank them down, and find her backside bare, not a slip of silk anywhere to be found, and color me happy. All the easier to find my way inside her.

"Shoes off," I order, and she does as I say, toeing them away before I wrap my arm around her and get rid of her pants.

The instant they're gone, I smack her backside. She gasps, and arches her back, thrusting her beautiful ass further into the air. Fuck, I love her ass in the air, but I have this realization that now is not that time. I feel like I've waited a lifetime for every moment I get with her. I want to see her, see everything she feels on her face.

I turn her to face me, but I'm not ready to shift the control, to let go of her submission.

Pressing her hands over her head, I order, "Hold them there."

Her lips are swollen, eyes heavy, voice breathless as she says, "I don't know if I can do that. I need to touch you."

"I promise you, I'll make it worth the wait."

"I waited a long time, Luke," she whispers. "Too long." Her voice trembles with emotions.

*Fuck.*

She might as well slice me open and gut me. Because it's the truth. It was too long. And I did that. I let that happen.

Guilt stabs at me and I release her hands, tangling my fingers in the silky strands of her hair, even as I pull her head back, and drag her mouth to mine. "No more waiting," I say, and already she is touching me, wrapping her arms around me, her breasts pressed to my chest. She is delicate and soft against me, a thorned rose, beautiful and strong, *my* thorned rose.

Holy hell, this is what I needed, not the games.

I deepen the kiss, drinking her in, my tongue licking deep, and I swear I could drown in the taste of her—all sweet and womanly—and it wouldn't be enough. Her hands, as soft as her body, press under my T-shirt, shoving it up and I reach behind me, dragging it over my head. I've barely tossed it aside and she's stroking my cock through my jeans, and I groan with the impact, I am hot and hard, and I might break the damn zipper. I set her back from me, lean her against the wall and at least for now, she waits for me, watching me with hungry eyes, and giving me just enough time and space to get naked.

Just enough.

I set my gun on the bed, and start undressing but the minute, and I do mean *the minute*, my pants are gone she's off that wall, reaching for me, and me for her. I catch her to me, sliding my hand under her hair and kissing the hell out of her. My hands slide and press down the seam of her backside, fingers exploring her intimately and low, before giving her another smack on that gorgeous ass.

Our mouths part and eyes meet and we both smile. It's an us moment, the way we can go from intense, dark, and insane for each other and manage to smile in the middle of it. I drag her mouth back to mine and say, "God, I love you, woman."

"Show me," she challenges, and just that easily we're back to that dark intensity.

I kiss her hard and fast, and then scoop her up, cupping her backside even as her legs wrap around my waist. I close the small space between us and the bed, lying her down on the mattress, and following, my body framing her body. My cock is between her legs, wet heat slick against my hard body, and oh hell yeah, I want to slide right in and fuck her until I can fuck no more.

But for a moment, we just linger there, the air thick around us. The push and pull of her need and mine colliding, a living breathing being in the room.

I lean in and trace her lips with my tongue. "Where would you like me to lick you next?"

"Just fuck me. Please *fuck me now*."

"Where do you want me to lick you, Ana?" I press.

"Do it later. Fuck me now. I need you inside me. I mean you have a lifetime to lick me all over, right? You better. And you can. Everywhere. And I'll do the same to you, but right now—"

I kiss her, cupping her breasts, even as I grab my cock and slide it along the wet seam of her body, fully intending to tease us both. That doesn't happen. She is so damn wet for me, and it's so damn hot, that I press inside her. She lets out this sound that is sexy as hell— a moan that is almost a sob—like me inside her is everything she's been waiting for, and I'm not even trying to go slow.

I drive into her, burying myself deep and she murmurs, "Luke. God, Luke."

My name. Her lips. My cock buried inside her.

My version of heaven on Earth. Kill me now and as I said, I'd die a happy man.

Kissing her, I roll us to our sides, trailing my lips over her jaw, her neck, and her nipple. I suckle it, lick it, and repeat, my fingers sliding into her hair in a rough tug that brings her mouth back to mine. With our lips close, I drive into her, press left and right, and say, "I will kiss you all over, Ana. Many times in this lifetime, and it still won't be enough." My mouth slants over hers and we're burning alive. Pressing into each other, moving together, grinding our bodies, and yet, it's more loving than fucking.

Still, there is a desperation to us, a need to be closer, to hold on tighter, and it's Ana who shoves at my chest, pressing me backward. Ana, who climbs on top of me, straddles me and rides the hell out of me. And she's sexy as fuck up there, breasts bouncing, lips parted, body all over me. I hold onto her hips, thrusting into the press of her sex to my body.

She leans into me, hands on my chest, and when my fingers pinch her nipples, that look on her face—holy hell, that look. I drag her down, her full breasts pressed against me, my fingers tangling all kinds of ways in her hair, my tongue licking into her mouth.

That's when that sweet grind takes over, the urgent pumps of our bodies, that sends us right over the edge. She stiffens and buries her face in my neck. "Luke. I ah—Luke."

She goes still, and my fingers splay between her shoulder blades, holding her to me, her body spasming around me. I pull her down into my thrust, the quake of my body rocking me. There is nothing but me and Ana right here, right now, and when we crash into each other, melt into one big puddle of satisfaction, I hold onto her like I will never hold onto her again. I'd lay here like this forever if I could, but a weird, shuffling sound at the door has me jerking upward and taking Ana with me.

I'm on my feet, gun in hand, in about ten seconds.

**LISA RENEE JONES**

# CHAPTER TWENTY-THREE

## ANA

Luke's literally naked and pointing his gun at the door, and I swear my heart beats with such fierceness that the entire hotel must vibrate from its force. If this doesn't define our lives right now, I don't know what does. I scramble for my gun as well, not even sure I remember when I took it off or where it rests, and end up standing beside Luke. Both of us stare down at a red envelope on the floor, just inside the door. A small wash of relief washes over me, be it that we are now facing a piece of paper versus an attack, but I'm still on edge. The hotel usually doesn't place a bill in a red envelope.

"What is this?" I ask, softly.

"Trouble," he says. "Get dressed, baby," and he's already reaching for my clothes and handing them to me, running down a plan. "We grab it. We read it in case it tells us something we're better off knowing, and then we get the hell out of here."

"Agreed," I say, and I watch him set his weapon down, uneasy that neither of us has one in our hands, but we dress quickly, and the weight of my firearm in my hand is all that calms the racing of my heart.

Once we're fully put together, Luke glances at me and we share a nod before he grabs the envelope. He quickly backs away from the door and both of us step out of the line of ammo that might make it through the wall, at least as best as we can, considering the small room. Literally, someone could spray bullets and we'd be dead, but I cling to the idea that these people want that package. Without us, they feel like they won't get their hands on it.

Luke sets his weapon on the bed again and opens the envelope, removing a card that reads, "Invitation."

*You are cordially invited to the home of Michael Phillips for a cocktail party.*
*Wednesday night, eight pm.*

Michael, being Newman's father.

And the party is tomorrow night.

Luke slides the card back into the envelope. "I have a lot of thoughts about this, but the most important one is: how the fuck did he know where to find us?" I'd echo his sentiments, but he doesn't wait for my confirmation, punching in a number on his cellphone and letting it ring on speakerphone.

Blake answers on the first ring. "Obviously, we have a problem."

It's confirmation our team is at least not wholly in the dark. "Phillips slid an invitation to a party under the hotel room door. We're leaving, but we need backup."

"Smith is in your hallway, harassing the cleaning lady who was hovering around your door, which we now can assume was to place the invitation. Dexter is sitting in the lobby, at a table, drinking coffee. Give me sixty seconds to get him ahead of you and Smith in front."

"Copy that," Luke replies, and disconnects, sliding his phone into his pocket, before punching the timer on his watch. "Obviously the son wasn't the real buyer."

"Agreed," I say again, "and either Phillips didn't give us those five days to find the package and meet up at the ranch, or he's impatient."

His watch beeps our sixty-second alert, he kisses me hard and fast, and says, "I'll clear the path, then you stay close. I want you in front of me after I give the all clear."

I don't fight him on the front or rear of this exit. We both know either side of the path could be the one with trouble which is exactly why he got back up. We close the space between us and the door, and Luke opens the door, to curse. "Fucking Smith."

I step to Luke's side and literally, Smith is standing there. He's tall, with sandy brown hair, and friendly, but intense, eyes. "They know you're here," he says. "You might as well walk out with the calvary."

He's not really wrong.

Smith backs away from the door, an invitation for us to exit. Luke eyes me and motions me forward.

Nerves prickle, the hair on the back of my neck standing on end but there is only one logical way out of this room and it's forward, and soon I'm sandwiched between Smith and Luke. We start walking. I think at this point it's safe to say, we are all of the same cautious mind. Because the truth is, the invitation could easily have been meant to create a false sense of security when we leave this room. At any moment, bullets could fly with us as the targets.

**LISA RENEE JONES**

# CHAPTER TWENTY-FOUR

## ANA

*An invitation to die.*

That's what I feel like I'm holding in my hand, not an invitation to a cocktail party.

The idea that our team had no idea we were being followed rattles me. We are working with the best of the best, and none of us were good enough to know we were anything but invisible.

Luke pauses at the elevator and punches the call button. I stop behind him, feeling that punch almost as if a bullet hit the wall. Every second we're in the open, we're targets. Every second we're in this building, we're among enemies. The doors to the elevator open and Luke holds the door for me.

I step inside and he joins me, and at this point, the steel walls feel like our coffin. We can't get out of this hotel fast enough to suit me.

Smith doesn't join us—maybe he doesn't like the steel coffin either—but he does crowd the doorway, his presence a reminder that we're not the only ones at risk. We're all targets. Us, him, and Dexter, who is also nearby. And every single one of us needs out of here alive. I try to take comfort in the fact that these people want something they believe we can give them. However, they killed Jake. Who says they won't kill someone else to prove a point? It feels like every move we make could create a target on someone else's back.

"Dexter is waiting on you in the parking lot," Smith supplies. "The maid says some guy paid her five hundred bucks to shove the envelope under the door.

Translation, we were about as discreet as a hungry two-year-old." With that little tidbit of information, he steps out of the doors and allows them to close.

Luke punches the garage floor button and eyes me but says nothing. At this point, our enemies have proven resourceful. For all we know, we're being recorded which forces our silence, but my mind is racing.

How did this happen, is my question.

Kurt comes to mind, but he was drugged when we left The Ranch. But the possibility that, as already suggested by one of us—I'm not even sure who at this point—he was there long before our arrival and set-up surveillance seems possible. Of course, so does us being followed in and out of The Ranch. Our vehicles could be tagged. We can't leave the way we came.

Apparently, I'm not the only one with this mindset.

The elevator doors open and there's an SUV parked right in front of the car, with a tall, fit man with thick, dark hair, leaning on the door. He pushes off the vehicle and joins us. "I'm Dexter," he informs me, and then eyes Luke. "I borrowed this big bitch for you. Blake will handle the owners."

Translation, he stole it, but whatever it takes to get us out of here at this point. Whatever it takes.

Neither me nor Luke argue. Luke gives him a salute and we climb inside the vehicle. The problem now being that we could have eyes on us, and probably do. Luke appears of the same mindset, wasting no time pulling us out of the garage, and quickly doing what he needs to do to get us on a main highway. Of course, I'm looking over our shoulders every second, when Luke gets Blake on the phone and he begins guiding our path via street cameras.

In the meantime, I text Blake a copy of the invitation. "Got it," Blake confirms. "Keep driving. I'll text you your landing spot. More on all of this bullshit soon." He disconnects.

"Okay," I say. "Keep driving doesn't seem like much of a plan."

"Better we keep moving than sit still right now, as far as I'm concerned. Every damn time we plant ourselves, we end up with a surprise."

"Right," I say tightly because how can I argue the truth? "What was that back there?" I hold up the invitation. "What is this? And how is Kurt involved?"

"Michael Phillips has money. The kind that pays for the best of the best which I might add, could mean Kurt, but Kurt doesn't feel right." His lips press together a moment, before he adds, "This isn't his work."

"He's alive," I argue. "He's been alive. He's had plenty of time to set us up."

"To what end?" he challenges.

"He wants the package."

"If he's been watching us, which we have to assume to be the case, he has to know we don't have it."

"They all think we have it, Luke, which is insane considering we don't even know what it is. This takes me back to my point back in the hotel room. We need to regroup. We need to step back and regroup."

"We need to end this."

"How do you propose we do that when everyone else knows more than us? We need to shift the knowledge gap."

"That's right," he agrees. "We do." He grabs the card from the seat where I've set it and lifts it, his attention shifting between me and the road. "Phillips knows what we don't know. We just got an invitation to the encyclopedia of knowledge."

"Or a grave we're likely sharing," I counter.

His cellphone beeps with a message, he glances at it before he says, "Blake found us a place to stay. A house in Highlands Ranch but he wants us to hang back at least an hour, and when he tells us, to head in that direction."

It's too close to The Ranch for comfort in my book, but that has it's plus side, considering Kurt's there, and we still need a river of words flowing out of his mouth. "We don't have an hour to waste right now."

"We both need to eat. Let's go to that taco joint we love."

I give a nod and then glance over at him. He's staring ahead, seeming focused on the road, but I can almost hear him preparing for battle, and that battle is with me. He thinks I'm going to fight him over how we handle this party. He thinks I'm playing this whole scene scared, and maybe I am. I'm scared of him and how eager he is to rush head-on into this. I lost him once. I'm not losing him again. And once he's dead, he's gone forever.

# CHAPTER TWENTY-FIVE

## ANA

Fifteen minutes later, Luke parks us on a residential street about a mile from the restaurant which is located in Denver's Washington Park neighborhood.

"This is where we leave her," he says. "We'll find another ride."

It's a good plan, and soon we're hiking across the park, through the neighborhood itself, and winding left and right until we're both sure we're not being followed. I'm aware of Luke by my side, aware of him perhaps more than I've ever been aware of him. I never thought he'd be by my side again. I never thought we'd have a future together and I can only pray that if we make it through this, we will not allow the past, or the scars our enemies left on us through that past, to destroy us.

"I think we're good," Luke murmurs, glancing down at me, our eyes colliding, a punch of awareness laced with the tension between us.

We're at odds over how to move forward, but not where we want to be right now. Which is safe. And on the surface, I believe that yes, we are good, we are safe, we're not being followed, but of course, that's not wholly true. No matter how much lost in suburbia we are right now, we're being hunted. And we will remain hunted until we become the hunters. And clearly today, we have not done a good job of making that happen.

"For now," I say, "yes."

He tears his gaze from mine, and says, "Then let's go eat." He motions toward the cozy street that is our destination, and soon we're in the hole-in-the-wall restaurant we love, that will surely do our bellies right, even if everything else is doing us wrong. We enter the dimly-lit joint with open seating and head to the rear high top, sitting side-by-side where we both can see the door and shoot at it, too, if necessary.

Once we order, the nostalgia kicks in—the Mexican music, the scent of tacos, peppers, and cheese, the familiar neon signs on the walls. The table we used to always share. My belly clenches. We loved this place. We loved each other. We still love this place and each other, but if our enemies have their way, they'll divide us again. We can't let that happen.

In unison, almost as if we are both thinking the same thing, the two of us rotate to face each other.

"Phillips knows we're showing this invitation to our people," Luke says, already making his case to attend the party. "That's the point, isn't it? That we know we're safe, because he's given us proof that he invited us to this party. He can't just get rid of us, Ana. At least, not at that party."

"We both know it's not always that simple. A false sense of security can be a dangerous thing."

"Which neither of us would ever have."

"We just had sex in a hotel room in the middle of a warzone, Luke."

"It wasn't a warzone, and we didn't take the danger for granted. We just wanted each other, Ana."

I lower my voice to an urgent whisper. "We have to be more careful."

"Agreed, but that doesn't mean we walk away from the invitation."

My fingers curl into my palms and our drinks are placed in front of us. Luke thanks the waiter and I grab my diet soda and sip. My throat is dry and my mind is racing. "This entire situation does not make sense, Luke," I say, setting my drink back down. "If he's the buyer, inviting us publicly, it's like taunting the seller."

"Maybe that's what he wants. Maybe it's a message. You get me my prize or I'll get it myself. And as far as I'm concerned, I want the seller to get riled up. Then maybe he'll fuck up and show himself. One wrong move and Blake will find him. You and I both know you don't go into the cave to catch the bear. You lure him out into the open."

"Which is my point exactly," I say. "Attending the party is us walking into Phillips' cave."

"Phillips is the buyer, Ana," he reminds me. "Not the king, and as your father said, we need to get to the king."

Our tacos are set down in front of us and the scent is divine. Luke and I both turn our attention to our plates, at least momentarily. Once we've both finished off a taco—okay Luke finishes two—he smiles over at me. "I missed this place, but most of all I missed *this*. You and me, doing normal things even if we're only pretending things are normal right now."

"Me, too," I say, thinking of how empty life has been without him. "Me, too, Luke."

"We're going to get back to this for real, Ana. We'll get our men inside the party. We'll spend the next 24 hours researching."

"Which is fine and dandy," I say, "but we're never going to have time to find out everything Kurt can tell us. We have to get him to talk."

"He's been talking. He just hasn't told us anything that helps."

"What if we just haven't given him the chance, Luke?"

He considers me a moment. "What are you getting at, Ana?"

"We need to go talk to him again and this time, leave our anger behind."

"We aren't going back to The Ranch."

"Then we bring him here."

"Anyone who leaves The Ranch will be followed."

"Then we go to him," when he starts to object, I hold up a hand, "we take the tunnels. We get in. We talk to him. We get us all out."

"And if it's a trap?"

"We start shooting."

That's when a tingling sensation prickles the nerves at the back of my neck and my gaze jerks to the doorway where I find trouble standing and staring back at us.

# CHAPTER TWENTY-SIX

## LUKE

Ana's gaze jerks to the doorway and mine follows, but I see nothing but the door opening and shutting. My hand goes to her leg. "What is it?"

"I don't know," she replies. "I thought I saw—I thought I saw," she glances over at me, "my boss. But he's dead, right?"

"That's what we were told." I grab my phone and text Blake, asking him to check out the cameras on the street. He replies with confirmation, a location, and instructions. "We're clear to go to the safe house." I toss cash on the table. "Leave your phone." I set mine on the table.

"You think our phones are being tracked? I thought Blake had that covered?"

"He does, but it seems like everywhere we go, someone else has us covered, too."

"Please tell me you don't think this is a Walker insider."

"It's not, and I just exchanged messages with Blake. He says he's 99.99% certain our phones were not hacked, but since Parker was with us, he says we have to err on the side of caution. I have no idea what that means and I don't care. I just want us free of this shit." I toss my phone in my soda and she follows suit, doing the same with hers.

"Blake's digging deeper on your boss," I say. "I hate to think we're supposed to believe he's dead and he's not because this shit is getting deep."

"It looked like him," I reply, "and as Kurt use to say: if it looks like a rat, it's a rat. And if that rat makes your hair stand on end, shoot it."

"Well, let's hope he follows us now and we can take that advice." I motion to the back door where I lift a staying hand, while I poke my head into the back alleyway, and clear our path. Once Ana's on the street with me, we move quickly and silently, snag another vehicle rather easily this time—a sedan parked outside a strip mall store—and hit the road. I spend twenty minutes driving us around, both of us checking the mirrors.

When I'm positive we're not only clear, but that we're also not even around any street cameras, I drive us toward the safe house, which is another Airbnb. Turns out it's a mansion of a place in a ritzy neighborhood. We pull up to the gate and obviously, Blake is watching because they open when we pull forward. The garage is no different.

We pull into the well-lit space and the doors close behind us. I'm out of the vehicle before they do, watching for any little pest who might think to sneak in before we're locked into safety. The instant we're clear from behind, I'm facing the door. Ana meets me at the front of the car, and I move to the door, open it, and move inside a long hallway. I can feel and hear Ana at my back, aware of her and of the need to protect her. And while I have no reason to believe anyone would be here, not with Blake clearing our path, today keeps driving home the need to be cautious.

An archway appears in my path and I step beneath it and freeze.

Caution has proven to be my friend.

We are not alone.

# CHAPTER TWENTY-SEVEN

## ANA

I step to Luke's side to find my father standing on the other side of the kitchen island with Savage to his right and Adam to his left. And he's not tied up.

"Hi, honey," Kurt greets, as if I'm not wishing he was sedated right now. "It really is good to see you again. And Luke. I was thinking about this earlier, while you had me tied up and shit. These people tried to tear you two apart and then foolishly, which is good for us, brought you back together."

"What is this?" I demand.

"Before you get all fucked up in the head over him being free," Savage replies, and motions to a laptop that sits open on his side of the island, "take a gander at his SIM card data."

"That information," Adam adds, "along with a conversation with Kurt, tells us, he's on our side."

I draw in a breath and Luke's hand settles on my shoulder, a silent offering of support, his way of telling me that whatever comes next, is my call. There is a pinch in my chest at the idea of Kurt being legit, a good guy, the man who I saw as my father, rather than a liar, who hid his death to hide an array of crimes. But I don't let myself fully experience those emotions threatening to surface. Not yet. I need to know how to use them, I need to know which ones are allowed to be real, and which ones are the little girl inside me who just wants the man she once called father.

I step forward and move to the end of the island.

When I'm standing directly across from Kurt, I just look at him.

I still can't believe he's alive. I'm not sure if I want to hug him or shoot him. He arches a brow, which I assume means I've been staring for quite a long while, which I'd defiantly continue, but we don't have time for emotional drama and power plays. I jerk my gaze from his and drag the MacBook closer. I start scanning communications between Kurt, Kasey, and other people, who are just numbers, not names.

At some point, Luke joins me and sets a stool behind me. I climb on top and keep reading. A few minutes later, a cup of coffee appears and Luke is beside me again. I guess he left and returned. A glance around and it seems Savage and Adam are now at the kitchen table behind me. I've been too busy reading and swimming in a pool of my own emotions to notice. I glance at Luke, this man I love and lost, only to find again, and then across to find Kurt who is now leaning on the counter behind the island, a cup in hand. He always loved his coffee. Every morning as a kid I remember him in the kitchen with his cup, steam pouring from the top. Part of being an adult and a badass was drinking coffee.

For all his faults, Kurt was always present, always demanding more of me, and as I force my gaze back to my reading material, I land on a text exchange between him and Kasey.

Kurt: *Son, enough. You're going to end up dead.*
Kasey: *Let me deal with me, Kurt. Fuck off already.*
Kurt: *What about your sister, Kasey?*
Kasey: *She's an FBI agent. She loves to tell me that. She can handle herself.*

That statement pinches. I never, ever said "I'm an FBI agent" to Kasey to be better than him. I don't even remember saying that to him at all. I swallow hard and keep reading, with Kurt's reply: *She can't stop a knife coming at her back if she doesn't even know there's a backstabber in the room.*

Kasey: *You calling me a backstabber?*

Kurt: *They told me they'd kill her if I quit, Kasey. If the fucking shoe fits, it fits.*

Kasey: *Fuck you, Kurt.*

Kurt: *You really don't want to keep saying that to me, Kasey. I've about hit my limit.*

Kasey: *You're all about limits, Kurt. That's why you're teaching. Teachers teach because they can't do.*

*You're about to find out just what I can do. You've been warned.*

Kasey: *Fuck off, Kurt.*

Luke's fingers flex on my knee and I glance over at him, the look on his face telling me he's read what I've read. And he's as conflicted as I am right now. He reaches up and strokes my hair from my eyes. "There's no crying in baseball."

It's a quote from an old movie, *A League of Their Own*, and I know this man so well, that I know exactly what he's telling me. We don't always like how the game plays out, but there is no such thing as quitting. The problem is, I still don't know if Kurt quit on me.

I shut the laptop and stand up, stepping center to the island in front of Luke. "You should have told me you were alive, you asshole. You didn't even have to tell me what was going on."

Kurt is now at the island, his eyes lit in anger. "Get over it, Ana. I did what I felt like I had to do to protect you. What is it that I've always told you? You make the decision you think is right to save lives, and you accept the consequences after the fact and tuck them away without self-blame because they can't be changed."

"Only I'm not the one who made the decision. You did. And now I have to live with it."

"We both have to live with it."

"Kasey is dead. Maybe—"

"I get it, Ana. You want me to feel guilty. You want me to be destroyed by his death, and by your grief, but I'm not going to do either of those things. I believe I saved your life. And we've had enough discussions over Kasey. He might as well have pulled the trigger himself. Stop blaming me and Luke for what that little shit did to all of us."

I push off the island and back right into Luke, who's still sitting on his stool. His hands come down on my hips, and he steadies me. His touch is fire, yes, but it is also a warm blanket on a cold night, the gentle comfort of partnership something I lost, but I've found again. Just like I've found Kurt again. Tears pierce my eyes and I don't even think about what comes next. I round the island and Kurt is there to meet me, pulling me into a bear hug, holding me too tight, the way my father would the daughter he thought he'd never hold again.

He speaks into my ear, at my neck, for my ears only. "I'm sorry, honey. I really am. I just needed to protect you, the way I didn't protect your mom."

In all my life, I've never heard Kurt apologize for anything, but that reference to not protecting my mom, that's what gets me. I'm undone. I'm bawling like a baby. When I pull my shit together, and Kurt releases me, Luke is there, kissing me before he motions to the other room. "We're going to give you some time."

I nod, and in a moment it seems, it's just me and Kurt, sitting at the island, steaming cups of coffee in our hands. Two grown adults, catching up on old times while plotting the end of our enemies. That's what our family time looks like and it's a good thing. A really good thing. Something worth fighting for. Even killing for.

**LISA RENEE JONES**

# CHAPTER TWENTY-EIGHT

## ANA

I'm not sure how much time passes, or how long Kurt and I sit there and talk, but it's not a conversation about the holidays and tender memories. I want to know who, when, where, and why all of this took place. I'm in that drilling mode, when Luke reappears in the doorway, eyeing me for approval before entering.

I motion him forward and he stops on the opposite side of the island where Kurt and I are presently sitting. Kurt eyes Luke and offers him his hand, and the two men—the two most important men in my life—share a strong handshake. And I believe we're stronger for it, too. We are only as strong as we allow ourselves to be together, at this point. And considering our history, which runs long, wide, high, and deep, it's a powerful connection.

It's also a surreal moment, having Luke and Kurt come back together, one I don't expect to punch me in the chest, and yet it does just that and more. I'm both comforted by their return to my life and terrified of the moment, they could be stripped away again. Terror is not a good place to operate from, and I've found knowledge to be the best way to offset that unhealthy emotion. Which, of course, was why I wanted to step back and dig for answers before we attacked. But I also want this over.

"I just spoke to Blake," Luke informs us.

"And?" Kurt asks as if Luke is reporting to him.

There's a slight hitch to Luke's lips as if he's amused by Kurt's take-charge attitude rather than irritated.

"He's certain, Mike, Ana's boss is dead. He says that's not in question."

Kurt's brows knit together. "Was that ever in question?"

"I thought I saw him at a restaurant," I explain, and then to Luke, "If Blake's right, then how do I explain what I saw?"

"Mike had a brother," Kurt replies. "Funny thing, too. He works for the Denver Lions football team which is owned by Newman Phillips's father, Michael Phillips." He forms a circle in the air with his finger. "It's all connected, just how deep? Where, oh where, is our king? I can't wait to kill that fucker."

"Mike's brother looks just like him, too, Ana," Luke adds, and uses a cellphone he's clearly acquired to show me the shot.

I stare at the man so like Mike and give a choppy nod. "Yeah, that's who I saw at the taco joint. So, he works for Phillips, and Phillips invited us to a party."

Kurt draws that circle in the air again. "Interesting how this all comes back to Michael Phillips."

"He's got to be the real buyer," I inform him, standing up and setting my coffee in the sink before moving to the end of the island to have a better vantage point with both men. "That's where we've been going with this in our heads."

"Think about this," Kurt counters. "Mike worked for the big guy. He replaced Maverick. What are the odds that Mike's brother worked for the buyer of one package versus the big guy himself?"

"Okay," I say, trying to work this out in my head. "Then maybe Mike's brother worked for Phillips and he was the one who told Phillips that Mike could help him acquire a treasure."

"Maybe," Kurt says, sipping his coffee. "Or maybe there's more to it than that."

Luke leans on the island and studies him. "You think Phillips is the king?"

My gaze lands on Kurt's. "You do?" I don't give him time to reply. "Then why risk exposing himself to us?"

"Maybe he thinks the safest place to be is in your face, pretending he's something he's not, like say, a buyer, who's on your side." He taps the counter. "That invitation they shoved under your hotel room door is our chance to kill him."

"We don't know he's the king," I argue. "We can't just kill him."

"I can," he argues. "I absolutely fucking can, then I'll disappear into the night again if that's what it takes to make this end."

"If you do that again, I'll find you, Kurt. And I might just have you arrested."

"Do what you want, baby girl, but if I find out that man is the king, he's dead. He fucked with my family. You don't fuck with my family, which is a testament to why I'm here right now."

I have so many emotions right now, that I stuff down deep, in that place inside me that allows me to do my job in the most gruesome of moments. My eyes meet Luke's. "How closely has Blake looked at Michael Phillips?"

"Close enough to agree with Kurt. He sent me the data he collected. He thinks Phillips might just be the king."

"Then we're walking into the lion's den, in all kinds of ways."

"But the lion," Luke says, "as strong as he may feel, is weak. And he's weak because he's money hungry, translation the package, and he still believes we're the ones who can give it to him."

Kurt leans his arms on the counter. "You know what inviting you to a big public party says to me?"

Funny how my perspective has changed. Now, the party invitation is no longer about us. It's about Michael Phillips protecting Michael Phillips. "He wants to appear to be our generous gift giver, and he wants the world to watch him do it. Because we won't kill him while the guests watch."

"Right," Kurt says, lifting his cup again. "Only he's wrong. I will, and then like I said—"

"You'll leave again?" I challenge as all those emotions I punched down low are rising in a wave of something that threatens to become quite messy. This is exactly why I rotate on my heels and march toward the door opposite the garage, and end up in the massive foyer with a round table, and high ceiling. *This house is too big*, I think. There are too many places for enemies to hide, and yet not enough for me to get lost in right now.

I step to the other side of the table, hug myself, and try to get right in the head.

I feel Luke even before I turn to find him standing in front of me. "Hey," he says, and when his hands settle on my shoulders, those emotions I'm battling shift and seem to reconstruct themselves into something calmer and far less disruptive, but no less intense. I love this man with all that I am, but life has taught me that love can be brutal.

But I can't say I'd be better off without it. That would mean I'm better off without Luke and that's simply not true.

"Smith and Dexter are about to arrive with a boatload of pizza, and I for one didn't eat enough to do anything but get angry. Therefore, I say, there's a private room and a pizza with our names on it."

"Is that the excuse you're giving me? I'm hungry so I'm angry?"

"Aren't you?"

"Hungry and angry? Why yes," I say. "I do believe I am."

He strokes my cheek. "He's not going anywhere. And neither am I."

My mind travels back in time and I try my hardest to remember the day my mother died. The day my father died. All I see is Kasey, walking toward the Jeep Luke had driven on the day he'd taken him overseas, to die. That's what it feels like. It was the day Kasey left and never came back. I'd felt it in these knots in my belly, even as I'd smiled and waved to Kasey as he'd climbed into the passenger seat.

Luke had kissed me then and said, "I'll see you soon."

"Take care of him," I'd insisted.

"Kasey can take care of himself, but I got his back, baby. You know I do."

And I did know. Because I'd known then what I know now. Luke loves me. And I love him. We would die for each other. The problem is too many people die on me.

I catch his hand. "Don't die on me."

He strokes my hair back from my face and stares down at me. "I won't make a promise I can't keep, but, baby, I will fight to the death to stay right here with you."

That's when I realize the hypocrisy of my anger toward Kurt. I say I want the truth. Well, his death was a lie, his leaving again, well that's the truth. Kurt is not here to stay and therefore in his mind, nothing he does has consequences. It's a state of absolute freedom.

It makes him dangerous.

# CHAPTER TWENTY-NINE

## LUKE

The sound of Smith and Dexter arriving cuts my conversation with Ana short, but I don't plan to let it end with nothing more than "don't die." Ana's tough as nails, but beneath the steel raincoat, is a human being, and humans are inherently flawed. She has abandonment issues because everyone she loves has left her, and while I know she knows this, knowledge isn't a cure. It's simply a tool to move forward.

"We should go get that pizza," she urges, obviously senses my hesitation to leave things as they are right now.

"All right then," I murmur. "Pizza first. You second."

Her lips curve. "Was the hotel not enough for you?"

"Never," I promise her, and it's the truth. With Ana, nothing is ever enough and even a day away from her is too much.

I settle my arm over her shoulders and guide her around the center table, then into the kitchen again. Smith and Dexter have stacked pizzas up on the table to the left of the island.

"Ana," Dexter greets. "Good to see someone has Lucifer under fucking control again."

Ana's brows lift. "Was he out of control?"

"He's fucking nuts," Smith assures. "Always trying to get himself killed and shit, and us with him. Fuck, man, I earned a shit ton of money with that man, but I'm lucky I'm alive to enjoy it."

Ana glances up at me.

"I have no idea what they're talking about," I assure her, only I do. When I thought she hated me, I hated myself, too, but I would never have done anything to get these assholes killed. "They're all pussified," I say, walking to the table and eyeing the pizza choices. "Smith hates heights and Dexter just likes to bitch."

"I'm the pussy about to wire this house and keep your bitch-ass safe," Dexter replies. "So, fuck you to Texas and back."

I laugh at how easily he's riled up and grab a pepperoni pizza while Ana walks to the fridge where she finds two bottles of water and holds them up.

She uses her body to push the door shut and I watch as Kurt catches her arm, then leans in to say something to her. Her lips press together, lashes lower before she nods. Kurt seems to hesitate, but he releases her, and then Ana walks toward me. When she steps in front of me, she doesn't make eye contact, which tells me she knows if she does, her emotions will spiral.

For that reason and that reason alone, I motion toward the house. "Pick a room, baby. And we'll make it ours."

She moves forward and heads for the stairs, which we travel together, side-by-side, in silence. She still won't look at me. Once we're on the second level it doesn't take long until we end up in the main suite, which includes two yellow couches, that look kind of like eighties elegance to me. I set the pizza box on the entry table, shut the door, and as Ana steps further into the room, I catch her hand and turn her to face me.

"What did he say to you?"

She casts me in a tormented stare, one glistening with unshed tears. I flashback to the first time I'd seen Ana cry. It was six months into our relationship. She'd walked into the kitchen where I'd been making my famous spaghetti, which means removing it from takeout containers, and she'd gone right for the glass of wine I'd poured her. She'd downed the entire glass, which never happens with Ana. I'd pulled her to me and the minute her eyes had met mine, the tears had flowed.

"A five-year-old boy," she'd sobbed, and it's all I could understand. It's all I needed to understand.

I pulled her close and held onto her, and I didn't let go all night. She'd held it together, and dealt with the stepfather who'd abused and killed that boy, but what she'd seen had broken her. She had become my hero that day and I didn't think anyone but my pilot father, who fought for our country and made the ultimate sacrifice, could ever claim that title. If I hadn't loved her already, I would have fallen in love with her that night. She has always fought for those who cannot fight. It's a selfless way to live, but again, that steel raincoat has limits.

Tears stream down her cheeks and anger burns in my belly. What the fuck is up with Kurt? Why must he hurt her? One of my hands settle on her lower back and I meld her to me, cupping her face and tilting her gaze to mine. "Talk to me, baby."

"Nothing to say. He's leaving. The end."

"That's what he said to you?" I ask, surprised by this news. I thought Kurt was back to reclaim his life and his empire. The fact that he's not, tells me there's more to this story than meets the eye.

"Yes, but you know, I respect him being honest. I do, but I think this is all about him sacrificing himself Luke, and I can't let that happen. He's going to kill Phillips if I don't arrest him first."

"You don't have anything that supports an arrest let alone charges. He's powerful. You need an avalanche of evidence to pile on top of him to even think about going down that path."

"I get that Luke, but if I have even a hair of evidence against him, I'm going to arrest him to keep Kurt from killing him, I'm going to arrest him."

I want to fight her on this, to insist she put herself and us first, but I love her and her badge. I just had that very thought minutes ago. Damn it to hell. I release her and turn my back, walking across the room before I face her again. "He's not going to kill Phillips. He doesn't know if he's the king." It's a repeated thought. I get that. But it's a point that needs to be driven home.

"He's acting like we've given him confirmation of something he already knew."

"He wants Phillips to be the king to end this. That doesn't make it so. We'll deal with Phillips. And we'll control Kurt. We'll drug him the night of the party and let him bitch about it later." I close the space between me and her and pull her close. "If we don't let him do something stupid, he won't have to disappear again."

"You make it sound so simple."

"It's not simple, but this is." I reach for the hem of her T-shirt, fingers sliding to her warm, soft skin beneath.

She catches my hand. "Luke—"

I kiss her, swallowing her objections, and it doesn't take long before she's naked, laying back on the bed, and spread wide for me. I lick her nipples and tease her mercilessly with every intention of giving her no time to think about Kurt and who she might arrest. I take my time with her, drink in her sighs and moans, kissing a path to her belly, and, with her plea, lower.

I'm between her legs, my tongue licking her into submission. The problem is, though I know that while Ana is all kinds of submissive in bed, the minute she has an orgasm and puts her clothes on, she's anything but. As if she's read my mind, she's already panting, and grabbing my hair, bucking her hips against my fingers.

She's going to come, but I'm holding her clothes captive.

We're going to spend as much of the next twenty-four hours leading up to that party naked as we dare. That's my intent, but Ana's barely finished, squeezing the hell out of my fingers, when there is a knock on the door. Holy fuck, I love my brothers in arms, but can a man get a peaceful naked moment with his woman already?

Ana jerks to a sitting position, and scrambles for her clothes. I walk to the door, and creep it open, only to find Adam standing there. The grave expression on his face tells a story and I step into the hallway.

"We have a problem," he informs me.

"No shit," I reply. "What is it?"

"Kurt is missing."

I digest that as the punch of trouble it represents. "Holy fuck. He's going to go kill Phillips." I scrub my jaw. "He clearly believes he's the person behind all of this."

"He told us as much. Right now, Phillips is on a plane from Italy to the US, which on a side note, gives him an alibi for his son's murder. Whatever the case, he's safe. He won't stay that way if Kurt is after him."

He's right. If Kurt wants to kill someone, they might as well dig their own grave.

He's trying to protect Ana. I know this. But he's also going to destroy her in the process. And I don't know if I can stop it from happening. "I need to talk to Ana."

He gives a nod and I turn away, entering the room. I find Ana standing close, hugging herself. "What happened?"

I step into her, my hands settling on her arms. "Kurt is missing."

Her chin dips and a heavy breath escapes her lips. "You might as well have told me Kurt's dead. I'm never going to see him again."

# CHAPTER THIRTY

## ANA

The next day, the day of the party, nearly twenty-four hours after Kurt disappeared, we've not heard or seen anything of him.

I spend most of that time, working with the Walker team to research Phillips. Turns out, Dexter is almost as good at hacking as Luke, and with Blake and his team at a distance, helping as well, we uncover interesting tidbits about Phillips. There are connections to numerous people on the list of buyers, Darius left us. There are connections between Mike's brother and several buyers as well. But there isn't enough to conclude wrongdoing, certainly not enough to say that Phillips is the boss of all of this mess. But we have a plan. Savage and Adam have managed to work their way onto the catering team servicing the party, which apparently is an annual event Phillips holds for charity. Smith and Dexter, along with Blake and his team, will be doing surveillance. Apparently, Blake even has a few extra guys flying in to offer backup, just in case we need it.

It's a few hours before the party, when a boatload of dresses arrives for me, compliments of Blake. I choose a black lace sleeveless gown, that flares and hits just below the knees. It's fitted at the bust and kind of a conservative sexy but none of that matters to me. What matters is the flare, which makes a weapon easy to hide. I study myself in the mirror and decide I do really love this dress, which is actually more of the result of Blake's wife's shopping, not him. Same goes for the strappy black sandals. And the hair tools that have my hair shiny and sleek, and the makeup that allowed me to gloss up my lips and add a sparkle to them.

Luke appears in the doorway of the bathroom, a vision of hotness in an expensive blue suit, that not only turns his eyes into an ocean of blue, but fits him like it's custom. "You look beautiful, Ana. Too bad I can't take you to dinner and show you just how beautiful."

I step in front of him and run my hand over his lapel. "And you, sir, look like the hottest man I've ever known."

"Careful, baby, or we won't make it to the party."

"We can still run away and regroup." I say, but it's a joke. Mostly. We aren't running away, but I do have a bad feeling about tonight.

"I thought you didn't want to run away?" he challenges.

"Okay, smartass. We both know I never wanted to run away. And we can't step back anyway. Obviously, Kurt's not going to. I wonder if we'll get our weapons in the door?"

"Probably not, but Savage and Adam will be armed. I just talked to Adam. They're certain they'll slide right in, weapons and all, and ready to help us, and set our plan in motion."

The plan, I think, isn't much of a plan but it's all we have.

Savage is going to get up close and personal with Phillips's beautiful wife, Lily, who is twenty years his junior. That way, if we end up with a gun to our heads, she will, too. Savage volunteered for the job because he says, he's the one who'd really pull the trigger if he had to do it.

I don't believe he'd kill her just to kill her.

But I don't have to believe it. He's a scary-looking dude. He'll make Phillips and his wife believe it.

**LISA RENEE JONES**

# CHAPTER THIRTY-ONE

## ANA

We exit the front door to find a fancy, black BMW waiting for us. "What's this?" I ask. "And please tell me we didn't steal this one."

"Rented," Luke replies, opening the passenger door for me. "We want to blend in with the money there tonight."

I slide inside the car and run my hand over the leather console, the new smell of the interior telling me this was not a cheap evening prop. Luke climbs in beside me, smelling all masculine and wonderful, compliments of the Airbnb bath soap, but it's really all about his scent, his presence. They say we react to each other's scent, that it's part of our attraction to one another. I'm fairly certain I was turned on by this man in every possible way from that first night we met.

He hands me a phone. "This has an app downloaded on it. It's marked with an X. It's going to become the cloud for any phone you get close to. We hope. It's some new technology one of Blake's tech buddies created and obviously the reason he was worried about Parker and our phones. The hope is we can take over Phillips's iCloud and find out what he's really up to tonight. He obviously plans to have a conversation with us, which means opportunity won't be an issue."

"We hope that's all he plans."

"If it's going to get bloody, baby, it will be all over the papers. You know he knows we'll shoot a million and one photos of us at his place tonight. It's possible he really just wants the package and he believes we can get it for him."

"Yes, but how does he know we're involved at all?" I ask, and it's a question I should have asked before now.

"Well, we know your boss was involved. We know your boss had you monitored in hopes of finding the package. The links that connect us to Phillips are pretty tight."

He's right, again, of course, but everything about this night still feels wrong. And as Kurt always said, never make wrong right. He was talking about a gut feeling, and yet that statement applies to his plan for tonight. He wants to make murder right. But then, his entire life has been about murder, killing for the government, and making wrong right by way of killing. That bothers me when I think too hard about it, which is why I don't think too hard about it, ever.

There are things that are not gentle, or sweet in this world, but are sometimes necessary.

I need to remember that.

*And so does Phillips*, I think because I am still Kurt's stepdaughter, trained to be his protégé. If it becomes necessary, I will bypass the arrest, and resort to my weapon as a resource, whatever that weapon may be, a fork if that's all I have handy. Tonight, I have to go into this and say that I will do what I have to do, especially if it means protecting those I love.

# CHAPTER THIRTY-TWO

## LUKE

The property is gated, in the middle of acres of trees, a true Colorado mansion.

At the entrance, we are required to show our invitation and IDs, before we're allowed to follow the long drive to the house. A valet waits for us there, and I catch Ana to me and kiss her. "Stay close."

"Don't worry if I don't. I know how to bring a man to his knees."

I laugh and release her as both our doors are opened. I exit the car and toss the keys to the valet. "She's new. Be gentle with her, or I won't be with you."

The redheaded dude smirks as if saying "fuck you" because he plans to drive the hell out of it. I step in front of him and stare a few inches down at him, putting on a show, of course. "If you think I can't find you, you're wrong."

His cheeks ruddy up and he quickly, says, "Yes, sir. I'll take good care of her."

"See that you do." I glare at him for impact and then round the car to join Ana, catching her hand to mine.

"Such a showman," she says. "I'm impressed."

I wink at her and we start the climb up several levels of stairs, walls of windows supporting the mansion with a red door to our destination. We reach it and yet another doorman greets us. He checks our invitation and then allows our entry. Once inside, a big bulky dude in a suit, with a buzz cut, and a dog face, awaits. Ex-military. I think. I know the type. Power hungry, and then some. He motions to a room to the left.

"You'll need to step into our security booth and be cleared for entry."

He means searched and no way in hell is anyone putting hands on Ana. Ana steps in that direction and when I try to follow, the man holds up a hand. "One at a time."

"She's not going alone," I state.

"I'm fine," Ana replies. "I promise."

I hesitate and then step up to dog face. "If anyone touches her inappropriately, you'll find out how little skill you truly have."

He smirks. He has no idea how unfounded his cockiness is, but based on how this night is starting, he may find out sooner than later. He surprises me though and says, "Go with her."

"Good decision," I state, but I'm fairly certain he's been told not to let us leave and he feared that might be exactly where this was headed.

Ana crosses to the room and enters. I follow and the man at the door shuts it behind me. There's a curtain, and he points, "You first," to Ana.

Ana glances at me and steps behind the curtain. I'm not about to allow her back there with some pervert alone. I step behind her and my eyes go wide when I find Kurt, wearing a suit, and acting like staff.

"Sir," he says sternly. "One at a time." He is the one winking at me now.

I don't know if I should be thankful that he's here, or wrestle him to the ground before he does something stupid. I step back. I can hear their hushed whispers, but make out nothing. Ana finally reappears, and says, "All clear. Your turn."

I search her face and find her read calmer than before she saw Kurt, the exact opposite of what I expected considering his vow to kill Phillips. I round the curtain and face off with Kurt. He hands me a note. I open it and read: *I am not going to kill Phillips here with all these people around. When have you known me to be that damn stupid? But I was not taking the chance of being drugged. I had to be here to protect Ana. That was non-negotiable.*

I ball up the note and hand it back to him.

Kurt has a theme going on that works for me.

He wants to protect Ana and this time he did it right.

By being present.

**LISA RENEE JONES**

# CHAPTER THIRTY-THREE

## ANA

We exit the main foyer of the house with our weapons intact, thanks to Kurt, and enter a spectacular room with a red bar to match the door, with guests in fancy garb milling about, many of which hold champagne glasses. A waiter offers us our own glasses and we wave him off. A clear head and empty hands work in our favor. A wall of windows presents us with a swimming pool, which is obviously heated considering this is Colorado and almost October, and it's filled with crystal blue water. There are levels above us, cool, modern stairwells that allow travel beyond where we stand.

I assume we will be watched and tormented by said watching for some time and I plan to make it work by meeting as many people as we can, and digging for information. I motion to an important-looking man—forty-something, sandy brown hair, an expensive watch, and suit—with a crowd around him that is clearly trying to please him and gain his good graces. "Target number one," I say, and start walking.

Luke falls into step with me and it's right when we step into the circle that I spy Savage out by the pool, talking with a familiar face. He's standing with Phillips's wife, holding a tray, while she smiles up at him, flirting up a storm with an ex-assassin who is also a happily married man. She will get nowhere with this exchange but we might just get everywhere.

I exchange a look with Luke, who smirks his approval for Savage's fast action. We're ready and waiting for confrontation. Bring it. Bring it *now*. But it's not now. It's an hour later, and way too much schmoozing when a tall, bulky man in a suit, steps in front of us.

"Mr. Phillips would like to see you both."

My heart begins a drumroll in my chest, followed by what feels like a tap dance, but on the outside, I'm cool and calm. "Nothing like special attention from the Mr. Phillips," I say smoothly.

Luke says nothing, but his hand settles possessively on my lower back and I swear I can feel his heartbeat in his palm. Or maybe that is still the tap dance of my own heart, working its way through my body, and into his. Whatever the case, it's showtime. My phone is in my purse at my hip, while my weapon rests on my thigh. I'm equipped and ready to meet Michael Phillips, who may or may not, be a friend. He also might be the king. Translation: *our enemy.*

# CHAPTER THIRTY-FOUR

## LUKE

We end up on an elevator with the big buffoon standing in front of us. I reach into my pocket and check my phone, which is presently downloading his data. That means Blake is already scouring it for information. I'm loving this shit while it works for us, but this is dangerous territory that could backfire if reversed one day. We end up on the third floor, when our guide boy steps into the hallway, with his shoulders all pulled back like a slingshot. He has no idea how much it weakens him, from front to back.

But hey. Better for me if I have to pick a spot to make him hurt.

Or die.

Whatever I need to do, Ana is walking out of here as beautiful and untouched by anyone but me, as she came in here.

Slingshot leads us to the left, toward a double red doorway, which is guarded by Adam. How he made that happen, I don't know, but my respect for him just continues to climb higher and higher. As for the doors, someone is superstitious, and I like those people as targets. They find a false sense of comfort in all the wrong things, like their money. I already know Phillips uses money as power, which isn't stupid. Money is power. Just not always the right kind to save your life. Slingshot knocks on the door and it opens.

He steps back and motions us forward. I resist the urge to eye Adam, and to capture Ana's hand that she might need to reach for her weapon. Side-by-side we step under the massive archway that is just one of the doors. We're now looking into an office with views of the pool with the mountains as a backdrop. Sitting at the desk, that is centerstage is Phillips, and he's not alone. There's a bodyguard to his right, standing tall and punching us with a stony headlight stare.

Phillips who is fifty-five, but looks younger, is fit, with salt and pepper, thick hair, and a piercing gaze. He surprises me by standing to greet us, rounding the desk to meet us on this side. Ana and I focus our attention on him, but I have one eye on the guard and an awareness of Slingshot at my back. But Adam is at his. Adam is our ace in the deck. But then so is Savage. Two aces are better than one.

"Welcome," Phillips greets, offering me his hand, not a blink of sadness, pain, or remorse present over his son's death.

I accept his hand and he presents a strong grip, but not too strong. It's practiced. The kind of shake that says I'm your equal but not above you. I don't believe that to be what he feels, but I respect his ability to deliver the message. "Good to meet you, Luke." He turns his attention to Ana. "And the lovely Ana, who manages to be both as beautiful as she is a badass. I've heard much about your father."

"Have you now?" she asks, and I notice the way she allows the "father" reference, without correcting him.

"I did my research on you two. Sit, please." He motions to the chairs in front of the desk and rounds them to claim his own. We all sit.

"I'm sorry to hear about your son," Ana states, clearly testing him.

His lips flatten. "Stepson from a prior marriage and we weren't close, but yes, it's tragic for her, I'm sure.

And pardon me if that sounds cold. We men do have our own way of dealing with such things."

There's a hollow sound behind those words that tells another story. He is not as cold to Newman's death as he wants us to believe. "You researched us and followed us," I say, punching at him, when his mind is elsewhere, "Tell me why."

"We all know why. I want something Ana's brother had until his untimely death. The seller can't seem to produce it, and my insiders inside their operation tell me they once again believe you have it. I just want my treasure. I'm hoping we can cut out the middleman and I can pay you for it and move on."

"We don't even know what it is," Ana replies. "We just know everyone suddenly thinks I have it."

His eyes fix on Ana. "Why is that?"

"I have no idea. Kasey came home in a casket. It's not like he handed it to me or hid it at The Ranch. Believe me, I'd hand it over, if I could. I want out of this."

He leans in closer and studies her, then me, then her again. "I don't believe you."

"That doesn't change my answer," Ana replies coolly. "And continuing to come at us for something we don't have is a bit like putting a square peg in a circular hole. It won't work."

"It will if you blow up the hole," he comments dryly.

I decide I've had enough. It's time for answers. "Shouldn't you be grieving your son, rather than throwing a party?"

His gaze jerks to mine and his lips curve in a twisted smirk. "I could tell you that it's an annual event for a charity my son supported with all his heart."

I arch a brow. "But?"

"He became a problem, just as Kasey did for you."

I laugh and run a hand over my jaw. "Am I supposed to flinch?" I challenge. "Or is she? Not happening. But when we think about who's pissed at who, it sounds like you have an impatient buyer on your hands."

"Extremely impatient."

"I already told your *people*—because I assume the goons chasing us are, in fact, *your people*, that I'd find what you want. For the right price, that is, but I need to actually know what I'm looking for." I leave it at that. I've volleyed back to him, and now I wait, to find out if he's going to tell me he's the buyer or the seller.

"I get it," he states. "You want to stop playing games. I do, too, and that's exactly why you're here. To get to the facts. No more digging for answers. No more hiding the truth. No more middlemen. We're here, the three of us, just getting it all on the table. I'm the buyer. I'm also the seller. A man can't live on football alone. I deal in fine collectibles and occasionally one crosses my path I want to make my own. This is one of those times. I want this prize for my personal collection. You already said you'd get it for me. You have one more day to deliver it to The Ranch, as promised."

And there it is. His confirmation that he was the one chasing us, and his men killed Darius, Jake, and who knows who else. Kurt was right. Phillips is the king. "I need five days after you tell me what I'm looking for."

He tilts his chair back and studies me for a good sixty seconds before he says, "The Natilda coin, worth a cool one million dollars if sold, but priceless to a collector such as myself."

"Okay then," I say, unaffected by the naming of a coin, that means nothing to me, outside a means to an end. "Let's negotiate. We'll find it. You forget us."

"Agreed," he says, leaning forward. "But I'll need collateral." He glances at Ana and then at me. "She'll do."

It's an expected response, and one Ana addresses, meeting his stare as she says, "At least your wife won't mind."

His brow furrows. "What does that mean?"

"Well, she's so into Savage, and all. Did you know that Savage is an assassin, and while Kurt would argue differently, I personally believe he rivals his skill. He's also young and hot." She eyes me. "You too, honey."

"What she's saying," I add, "is that you might want to find out where your wife is right now."

Irritation flits across his face and he snags his phone from his pocket, punching in a number. "Where is my wife?" he demands, listening before he says, "Find her."

My phone buzzes with a text and I remove it from my pocket to find a message from Blake, a well-timed photo of Savage talking to Phillips's wife. His wife is touching Savage's arm and staring at him as if he's a god. I set my phone on the desk. "He doesn't need a weapon to kill her. And he's not the only one with his skill set in the building right now. We can make this event get dirty fast. We'll get you the coin, but we're walking out of here alive and together."

He snaps up my phone, studies the photo, and sets it down. "She doesn't matter to me," he states, but the set of his jaw says otherwise. "But get the fuck out. You have three days to get me what I want. No more. And just to be clear, Ana, I own the FBI. Try to cross me and the body count will pile up."

I don't reply. I don't smirk, though it's tempting. I don't taunt to lion in his own den. Instead, I offer Ana my hand and stand, taking her with me. "Well, we better go, then," I say, meeting his stare. "Before the body count adds up." With that, I place Ana in front of me, walk toward the door, and make sure it's me who gives Phillips and his bodyguard my back.

# CHAPTER THIRTY-FIVE

## ANA

The minute we're inside the BMW I turn to Luke. "How's Savage getting out of there? And why didn't I think about this until now?"

"He's resourceful. He'll get out."

I want to find comfort in those words, I really do, but we just made Savage a target. And I was so small-minded I never even thought of how he exits the party and manages to do it alive.

"Adam is in there with him," Luke adds. "Smith and Dexter are present. And none of them will let Kurt kill Phillips."

"Lord, help us," I say, understanding coming to me, "we just left Kurt inside that house with the man he wants to kill."

"He doesn't know he's the king, as he calls him," Luke replies, pulling us down the driveway. "I don't know what he said to you when you saw him," he adds, "but he reminded me he's not dumb enough to go at Phillips in that public of a setting."

I cling to those words, I do, but I'm also watching our rearview, making sure we leave the property without a tail. Exiting the gates is only step one, but it's a big one that I wasn't sure Phillips would allow. Once we're on the main street, we get the heck out of the area, and then and only then, does Luke call Blake. "Talk to me," he says when Blake answers.

"You got his data," he tells us. "I'm working it now. What do I need to know?"

"He's the guy," I say. "The head of all of this. He's looking for a coin called the Natilda."

"He says it's for his personal collection," Luke adds. "But he's antsy to get it in a way that tells me he has a powerful buyer."

"Who obviously wasn't his son," I add. "Darius somehow thought his son was the buyer. I have a feeling he was tricked, and that's how he ended up dead."

"Sounds like it," Blake replies. "You two drive. I'll work the data."

"What about Savage, Kurt, and Adam?" I ask.

"They can handle themselves," Blake assures me. "Adam has eyes on Kurt. He won't leave without him. More soon." He disconnects.

We spend the next fifteen minutes, ensuring no one can follow us to the house. When we're finally there, Luke pulls us into the garage, and we enter the house to find Kurt standing with Savage and Dexter around the island.

I don't know who I'm more relieved to see—Kurt or Savage.

"That cloud app worked," Dexter informs us. "Blake's working on the information now."

Luke shrugs out of his jacket and tosses it on a chair by the table while I step to the end of the island. "I can't believe you were there," I chide Kurt. "You didn't even use a disguise."

"They all think I'm dead, baby girl. Hiding in plain sight makes dumbasses confused."

"True that," Savage chimes in, popping the top on a beer and slugging a drink. "Those fuckers weren't well-trained. You'd think a rich bastard like Phillips would hire better talent."

"You shouldn't have been there," I continue, still focused on Kurt.

"I'm here now," he says, his eyes practically bleeding with the stubborn attitude I find there. "And I'm fine. Alive and well."

"Until you get yourself killed."

"He's a tough old geezer," Savage interjects. "Chicken shit who ran from me, but still a tough old geezer."

"I left before I was forced to hurt you," Kurt assures him.

"Old guys need naps," Savage rebuttals.

Kurt scowls and Luke cuts off the battle of assassins. "How'd you get out, Savage?"

"Adam spilled a drink on Phillips's wife. I escorted her to the bathroom and disappeared. Not before she tried to take me into that private space alone, but nope. I'm a married man."

Dexter's phone rings and he holds it up. "Blake." He answers the line, listens for a minute, and then places it on speaker. "You have Savage, Kurt, Luke, and Ana in the room."

"Adam's in the surveillance van with Smith, waiting to see what Phillips does next," Blake informs us. "And now I'm going to tell you what I assume Ana and Luke already told you. Based on the cloud data, Phillips reads like the seller, not the buyer. He's the main captain of this ship."

"The king," Kurt replies. "Kill him. We kill at least the part of this operation that cares about any of us."

"Or we could arrest him," Blake replies. "Which is the preferred method of attack. But right now, I'm focused on how we control him to keep everyone alive. I believe that means we need that coin, or at least to make him believe we have it, which our team researched. It disappeared from a museum in Paris over a decade ago. Luke this comes back to you. What happened to that package?"

"Trevor had to have taken it," he says.

"And then he came to The Ranch," I interject, with a thought hitting me. "Wait. Can I see the coin?"

Luke pulls out his phone. "Googling it now." He punches a few buttons and then shows me an image. My lips part. "I ah," I laugh, a disbelieving laugh, "wow. Okay. Well. I know where it is."

# CHAPTER THIRTY-SIX

## ANA

My confession is out before I can stop it, a reckless move with Kurt's motives still at least a little in question. Luke and I share a look that says that and more, but Kurt isn't about to let that ride.

"I don't give two shits where it's at," he declares. "Tell them later. What I care about, is how we use that to our advantage. We can't hold the coin captive forever. He'll keep coming for us all until we come up with a way to make this work for us. This is one part of a bigger picture."

"I have additional information," Blake interjects, "but I agree with Kurt. One piece of a bigger puzzle. Based on the cloud download, I can confirm he's not looking for the coin to keep for himself. He has a buyer, and that buyer is someone who we don't want to piss off. He's widely believed to be a future world leader, who might come off as a nice guy, but the dude has a trail of bodies behind him."

"In other words," Luke replies, "Phillips is scared."

"Yeah," Blake confirms. "And I'm pretty sure from what I read tonight, he didn't kill his son, who is not his stepson, by the way. He's blood. I'm betting his buyer killed Newman."

"Okay, you have my attention, Blake," I say. "Who in the world is this buyer?" I ask, shaken by just how dangerous this situation has become.

"Louis Dubois," Blake replies. "And as I said, he's widely believed to be the future—"

"French Prime Minister," Kurt supplies, with a laugh. "Yes. Yes, he is. I know him."

"What does that mean?" I ask. "And is that good or bad? Does he like you or hate you?"

"I am part of the reason he's where he is today."

"You killed for him," Luke assumes tightly.

"Hell no, son, but I trained all of his private security and 'fixers' as he calls them. What they do with the skills I give them is not on me. Just like money, skills can be used for good or evil. No one asks when they pay the grocery store if they're going to use the profits for a good thing. Bottom line, if we're willing to give Louis the coin, he'll handle Phillips."

"Blake?" Luke asks. "How willing are we to give up a coin that belongs in a museum?"

"Based on the level of trouble Louis represents," he says, "give him the damn coin, but we need to know that equals safety for everyone involved."

"It will," Kurt assures us all, and he eyes Savage. "Some of us can do more than use brute force."

"Hey, man," Savage replies, "I can blow you up and put you back together, so you might want to keep me on your side."

"What comes next?" I ask. "Because Louis believes you're dead."

"I got this," he says, pulling a phone from his pocket, and punching in a number.

"What are you doing?" Luke asks. "Who are you getting involved?"

"Yeah, man," Dexter adds, pointing at him, "we talk before we act."

"Relax," Kurt replies. "I'm calling Louis to end this shit. And yes, I have his number. I kept all my contacts." He punches the speaker button and the line rings.

A man answers. "Bonjour."

"Louis, my man," Kurt greets. "Miss me?"

"Who is this?" is the thickly accented reply.

"Oh, come on, man, you know who this is. And you know I'm not going to say it and neither are you. It's me."

"That's impossible. You are dead."

"Come on, brother, don't make me say that nickname that chick from London had for you. I mean, I can. She also said you had really big—"

"Stop. Stop now. This still proves nothing."

"All right. Well, we both know it does. I have that treasure you're hunting. Just happened. One of those things. You know I'll never keep what is yours, but I will need a favor in exchange. Just a small one. Nothing you won't enjoy."

He's silent a moment. "I'm in New York. Come here. Let me see you face-to-face and know it's you. Then we'll see about favors and treasures." He hangs up.

Kurt eyes Luke. "Time to put on your pilot wings. We just need a plane you can fly."

"Done," Blake replies. "I'll see you at the airport." He disconnects.

Kurt's attention lands on me. "I hope you really have that coin. We'll be needing it now, not later."

"Right," I say. "Well, that's slightly complicated." I glance at Luke. "Can we talk?" I motion to the foyer and walk in that direction.

Once I'm on the opposite side of that table again, I face him, hugging myself. "I buried it with Kasey's body. It was in his pocket. I just—I thought maybe it mattered to him so I put it in his hand." My throat goes raw at what must come next. "We have to dig him up."

He steps into me, hands setting on my shoulders. "You okay with that?"

"Yes, I mean as right with it as I can be. But I really don't want to be there."

He studies me a moment and says, "Our guys can handle it. Dexter's a pilot. He'll fly it in separate from us. Unless you want me—"

I catch his shirt, fingers curling around it. "No. That would be torture for you. And I'd rather us just stick together. I think we're stronger that way."

He cups my face. "We are stronger together, Ana."

"And now I can see where you live, right?"

"I live wherever you live, baby. Surely you know that by now."

"Well, maybe we can live in New York."

"You want to leave The Ranch? What about your job?"

Phillips's words come back to me. *I own the FBI*, and while I don't believe that to be true, not on a widespread basis, I'm bothered by how easily my division became fodder for his money and power. All of it connects to a past I'm ready to leave behind. "I think I might be done with the FBI. You think Blake would hire me?"

"I know he will. If that's what you want." He kisses me. "We'll figure it all out."

*We.*

I replay that word in my head and while I can stand alone, I can be comfortable with me, just me, I really like me with him. I like the "we" that we have become again. And I am ready to fight to protect what has been lost and found once again.

# CHAPTER THIRTY-SEVEN

## LUKE

Dexter and Smith handle the retrieval of the coin.
Kurt, Adam, and Savage travel with us.

At present, Ana sits in the front of the plane with me, and what most people don't know, not even Kurt, I suspect, is that Ana knows how to fly a plane. I taught her. Is she officially licensed to fly? No. But could she in order to save a life, including her own? Yes. I made damn sure of it years ago now, which was partially because she was afraid of flying.

It's a control thing I understood then, as I do now. When you ride, there is no control. When you pilot, there is more control than there is on a highway in my opinion. Which is exactly why I offer Ana my seat now. "Take the wheel, baby. It will make you feel better."

She holds up her hands. "Not a chance. There are too many lives on the line. I'm not a pilot. That's you."

"Ana," I start but she quickly adds, "I know what you're doing, Luke, but I feel just as in control with you behind the wheel." Her eyes soften. "And there is no one else in this world I could say that to and mean it. Thank you for being my person. Because you are. You know that, right?"

It's right then that Kurt pokes his head into the cockpit. "How're we doing?"

"The coin will get there," I assure him.

Kurt kneels next to Ana. "And where exactly was it, daughter?"

She glances at me and I give her a nod. It's done. It's been done fifteen minutes ago according to the text Dexter sent me. "It was with Kasey. Now it's not."

"You buried him with the coin?"

"I didn't know it was 'the coin,'" she assures him. "It was just what he had in his pocket."

"In other words," I add, "Kasey was delivering an empty package or a package with a fake coin."

Kurt glances at me and then Ana. "It's almost like he had a death wish. You were never going to save him. Don't let digging up that coin stir up guilt that is undeserved. No matter how we try to understand, we never will. It was his time. We all have that time and when mine really comes, I won't be able to say I should have, or could have, done anything. Focus on you and making sure that's true for you, too." He glances. "Get us to New York. Let's end this." With that, he pushes to his feet and leaves the cockpit.

"He's right," she says, when the door to the cockpit shuts. "Let's just go get this done and start our new life. It actually feels like that might really happen."

"All right then," I say, flipping a switch on the dash. "Let's get the hell out of here, but for the record, you're my person, too, Ana." I wink, and call back to the cabin. "Sit your asses down and buckle up. I don't like most of you so this will be a bumpy ride and no, I'm not sorry."

Ana laughs and it's a perfect song cutting through the darkness of the past year.

A few minutes later, it's our plane cutting through the darkness of the night, but I keep the ride smooth. Because as much as we all want this to be over, I'd bet money that the bumpy ride isn't over yet. There's still a war ahead and we need our team ready to fight.

# CHAPTER THIRTY-EIGHT

## LUKE

We land in New York City on a private airfield owned by Walker Security.

Blake is waiting when we deplane, with Royce, the oldest of the clan by his side. Both are tall, dark, and big, but Royce brings a side of rough and tough to the mix. A man of few words, and an abundance of attitude. Meanwhile, Blake is one big "fuck" machine.

"Fucking great to meet you, Ana," he greets, shaking her hand. "Not fucking sure how I feel about you, Kurt," he adds, eyeing him. "Which is exactly why you're staying with Savage."

Savage joins us and says, "I have my syringe ready and waiting, old man."

"Chicken shit and his syringe," Kurt grumbles. "I need to be close to Ana. I'll stay with Luke."

"Not happening," I say. "Not until this is over and I know exactly where you stand."

"I've told everyone where I stand," he snaps.

"Show us," Royce replies. "That's the only reply that works."

And there you have it. The reason I respect the Walker brothers. They're honest men who are both warriors and friends. They also don't bullshit. Kurt scowls but pulls his phone from his pocket and punches a button.

"I'm here," he says whenever whoever he called answers. "All right. I'll be there waiting." He disconnects. "He'll come to me. He got me a room at the Continental Hotel under the name Todd Moore."

"And just that easily he took control," I say. "I don't like it."

"Me either," Ana replies, "but considering his track record I'm not surprised. At least it's a public property. It's feels safer than a private residence we can't access as easily."

At least, I think. And yet, I'm not comforted at all.

My gut is screaming like a stuck pig. Somehow, this is going to backfire. Exactly why I'm keeping Ana away from it. I catch her hand. Blake eyes me and seems to read my reaction. "I'll get him to the hotel. Savage will stay with him."

Savage grins at Kurt. Kurt is back to scowling.

As for me, I start walking, and take Ana with me.

# CHAPTER THIRTY-NINE

## ANA

Luke drags me toward a black SUV and I tug on his hand. "Wait. Luke."

He doesn't wait. He uses brute force to propel us both forward. "No waiting, baby. I have a gut feeling I don't like."

These are words I understand. We've had this conversation. A gut feeling is never ignored. It exists for a reason, but I'm struggling with the idea that if I leave Kurt here, I leave all semblance of control. But gut feelings win. I know this. I stop fighting him. I keep pace, and when we're inside the back of the SUV, it's Adam who slides into the driver's seat.

"Home?" he asks.

Luke catches my leg and drags me close to him, staring down at me as he says, "Yes. Home."

Everything inside me turns to mush. I've never even been to New York City, but yes, home. Because anywhere with Luke is home. I touch his face. He catches my hand, his touch warm as he kisses my hand. I melt for him right here in the backseat of an SUV.

His arm slides around my shoulders and I sink against his warm body. The vehicle starts to move and I glance out of my window to watch Savage and Kurt in what appears to be a heated exchange. I'm pretty sure those two are going to come to blows, and I'm not going to try to stop what can't be stopped. They're two freight trains with no breaks.

Luke laughs. Adam as well. "Gotta love Savage. He keeps things interesting."

I barely hear the words. Suddenly, I have nerves dancing in my belly, or perhaps ice skating on unsteady ice is a better description. I'm going to see the place Luke lives, and experience the life he created without me. Somehow that feels incredibly intimidating.

Almost as if Luke reads my mind, he cups my face and tilts my mouth to his, brushing his lips over mine, and then lingering there a moment before he releases me. It's his way of saying we're together in all things. It doesn't wash away the nerves, but it somehow stirs more of a feeling of anticipation than uncertainty.

\*\*\*

Twenty minutes later, we pull up to a high-rise building, and Luke opens the door, offering me his, "Welcome to your second home, baby."

My nerves do jumping jacks, and my palm presses to his, heat and tingly sensations sliding up my arm. He guides me to the ground and the chill of the night is damp and wet, so unlike the dry cold of Colorado, driving home the distance that was between us and not so long ago now. We enter the lobby which is all about black shiny tiles. Luke waves to the doorman and his arm is back around my shoulders.

Once we're in the elevator, Luke punches in a high-level floor, and pulls me close. "I know you, Ana. You're going to make this like some sign our lives are too separate to be together, but that is so far from the truth."

My hand settles on his chest, and his heart thunders beneath my touch. He's nervous, too, and this is really silly. We love each other. Nothing about me going to the place he lived without me changes that. "I know that, Luke."

"Do you?"

"Yes," I say firmly. "Yes, over and over."

The elevator dings and so does my heart, as silly as that would sound to someone. Luke pushes off the wall and takes me with him. "Come on, baby." He catches my hand and leads me out of the car, and down the hallway.

At the door, he hesitates. "I bought it thinking maybe one day, you'd come here, and want to stay." He cups my face. "It's not a ranch with horses, but—"

I push to my toes and kiss him. "It's already perfect."

He draws a breath and sets me in front of him, before punching a code into a panel and then opening the door.

**LISA RENEE JONES**

# CHAPTER FORTY

## ANA

I walk inside the apartment to find a massive room with windows, luxurious wood finishes, bookshelves filled with hundreds of books, a stunning kitchen island and so much more. It's warm and welcoming, and expensive. I turn to face Luke as he shuts the door and locks it. When he rotates to face me as well, the heat between us punches like fire, no ice in sight.

He catches my hand again, and walks into me, his hand on my hip. "I hated every moment I was here without you, Ana."

"I hate the idea of you here without me," I reply, and every part of me is alive in ways I was never alive when we were apart. "I don't want to know what that feels like again."

His hand slides over my hair and his mouth lowers to mine. "Marry me, Ana."

I laugh a throaty laugh. "You have already asked that. I already said yes."

"Say yes again, right here, right now."

"Yes," I whisper. "Over and over, yes," I add, repeating the words I'd used in the elevator.

His lips brush my lips and then he leans in and kisses my neck before he murmurs, "Again."

My teeth scrape my bottom lip. "Yes."

He scoops me up, lifts me, and my arms wrap around his neck as he starts walking. I bury my face in his neck and just inhale him, and it's still not enough. I just can't even believe we're together again, and I haven't even had the time to process the reality of it. I hold onto him, and I vow never to let go again.

At the top of the stairs, Luke enters a room and flips on the light. It's really only then that I process the fact that it's dark outside. I don't even know if I'd know the day of the week if I didn't stop and think.

Luke sets me down at the foot of a massive king-sized bed with pillars and a heavy wood construct. He doesn't undress me though. And I don't undress him. We undress together, and then end up there at the end of that bed, naked and staring at each other, a world of emotions and history between us.

When we come together, every touch is tender and yet a blast of lightning, igniting my body, and my heart. We go down on the mattress, and there is no rush. There is no divide. There are no boundaries. We touch each other. We kiss each other. We savor every moment, as if it might be...the last.

# CHAPTER FORTY-ONE

## ANA

We're naked, lying face-to-face, and talking, when Luke's cellphone rings from somewhere on the floor. Both of us sit up, and adrenaline zips through my veins. This is it. I know this is it. By the time Luke is standing and holding his phone, I'm reaching for my pants I put on back in Denver, with no luck. Where are my pants?!

"Closet," Luke says. "Blake's wife brought you clothes." He answers the call on speaker. "Yeah, Savage?"

"Louis is downstairs in a limo, waiting on Kurt to come down. Get here now." He disconnects.

I'm already climbing over the bed for the fast path to the closet. In ten minutes, I'm in jeans, boots, a tank, and a hoodie with a gun at my waist. We're about to exit the apartment when Luke catches me to him and kisses me hard and fast. "This is our apartment now, not mine."

"Yes," I say, warmed by his insistence, and determination to make his home my home. "I want to be here, not there. I want to go back, pack up, and just come here. Like tomorrow. Or when this is over. I just want to be here." I surprise myself with just how vehemently I say those words. I'm done with The Ranch and the FBI. I feel it in my bones.

"Tomorrow," he agrees, setting me free.

A few minutes later, we are on the street in the SUV with Adam. "You still have the coin?" I ask.

"Dexter has it," he replies. "We decided we didn't want you two with it on your persons, which means it can't be with me because I'm with you. If Louis wants it, we need a trade of sorts. Safety for the coin."

"It's his promise of protection," Luke replies. "I don't like that view."

"Kurt knows him," I say. "I don't think he will want to cross him."

"Let's just hope Kurt isn't working with him and fucking us over."

It's a brutal thought, but one we have to consider.

Adam pulls us into traffic and Luke and Adam's cellphones buzz with a text. Luke reads his and then shows the message from Savage to me: *The cellar. Lower level.* And address follows.

A cellar feels way too much like a grave to suit me right now.

# CHAPTER FORTY-TWO

## LUKE

Every part of me wants to make Ana skip this meeting, but I know my woman. She will never find peace in anything that goes right or wrong, if she's not present. But as we pull to the back alleyway behind the cellar, as instructed, I battle my protective side with Ana. *Kurt will never let her get hurt*, I tell myself. I believe he loves her.

Adam parks the SUV in front of the rear door, and exits. I kiss Ana, and do the same. She follows and steps to my side. Turns out, we don't have to go inside at all. The door opens and Kurt exits, followed by several men in black, packing obvious weapons. Another SUV pulls across the drive, blocking entry or exit, which makes me twitchy.

Kurt halts and the door behind him opens again. A tall, thin man appears, and you might as well call his suit "money" it's so obviously expensive. I motion to Ana and we step in front of the two men.

"I am Louis," he greets, and flashes Ana a smile. "You are right, Kurt. She is as lovely as her mother, or even more so." He holds up a hand. "No offense."

Ana tenses ever so slightly and I know she's thinking what I'm thinking. Did this man have anything to do with her mother's murder? But I dismiss that idea instantly. Kurt loved her mother. He talks about her. He softens with her name on his lips.

Louis offers me his hand. "Lucifer," he greets. "I've heard much about you. I need you to fly my fleet for me, but I hear I can't pay you enough to win you over."

"You'll win a favor of my choice, not yours, if this goes my way today," I assure him.

Louis eyes Kurt. "You were right. He holds nothing back. I like him for Ana." He winks at Ana.

"I didn't know I had the coin," Ana tells him. "It was on my brother's person when he died. I thought it was just a coin. I'm sorry if this caused you distress." She delivers this with the sweetness of a woman who would never kill a man. But she would. She'd kill him right now if she thought it necessary.

His eyes soften on her. "I appreciate that. Where is it now?"

"I gave it to Walker Security to protect, for the both of us. Michael Phillips seems quite desperate."

His lips twist. "Is he now?" He doesn't wait for an answer. "I need proof you have the coin. If I get that, I'll end your trouble with Phillips."

"How can we be sure they're ended?" I ask.

"You'll be sure or you won't hand me the coin," he replies.

Adam presents his phone with a photo of himself holding the coin. Louis eyes it and then Kurt. "You, my man, always come through, even from the grave." He retrieves his phone from his pocket and punches in a number. It rings on speakerphone. He allows us to hear Phillips answer the phone before he says, "You are to leave Ana and Luke alone until further notice, and that means anyone they even speak to, let alone know intimately. Understand?"

Silence fills the line several beats before Phillips says, "That's complicated."

"It isn't complicated at all," Louis replies tightly. "No contact. No harm. The end." He disconnects and says, "Once I have the coin, one of my men will visit him in an unforgettable way, not that this is even necessary. When will I receive my treasure?"

"Tonight," Adam replies. "It's in our office safe."

Louis's eyes light. "Well take me there now." He offers Ana his hand. "A pleasure, my dear. You will be safe." He inclines his head at me and motions to Adam. "I'll ride with you." He then waves at his guards, who follow him to the SUV.

Kurt steps closer. "I'm going with him. I'll call you when it's done." He starts to walk away and Ana catches his arm.

"Don't disappear."

"I won't leave you in the dark ever again." With that, he dislodges her hand and heads to the SUV.

When the SUV blocking the driveway moves, and Adam pulls out of sight, Ana and I face each other. "He's going to leave."

"There's more to Kurt's story than we know, baby. There always has been. But maybe, just maybe, he doesn't want to be at the beck and call of men like Louis. And who can blame him?" I stroke her hair. "Let's go home, and tomorrow, we'll figure out what comes next."

"We have no car."

It's right then that another SUV pulls in. "Now we do. We'll always find a way, baby. Don't you doubt it."

We load up in the vehicle with Dexter driving.

It's an hour later, when we're sitting at the kitchen island eating pizza that my cellphone rings, with Kurt on caller ID. "It's done. I'm going back to Denver in the morning. You going to fly me there?"

I glance at Ana, knowing she's not letting him out of her sight. "I'll see you at the airport." I disconnect, expecting Savage to coordinate details.

"Well?" Ana asks.

"It's done. And I just promised to fly Kurt to The Ranch tomorrow."

"Good," she says. "We can get me packed up to move here."

"You sure about that?"

She glances around her and says, "I'm home. And I love my new home." She picks up a slice of pizza. "I'll have another slice to celebrate."

And I want to celebrate with her, too, but something about all of this just feels too tidy.

My damn gut is screaming like a banshee.

# CHAPTER FORTY-THREE

## LUKE

I wake with Ana in my arms and in my bed and news that snow is expected in Denver. I love flying into a snowstorm, more than I probably should, especially early season when I haven't done it for a year. In other words, it's a perfect morning or would be, if not for the fact that gut feeling just won't go away. I also have a message from Savage from about three am. Apparently, he and Kurt played poker with the guys all night. Kurt wants to leave later in the day, which works for me. I need time to figure out what is bothering me. What I get is time with Ana, sharing breakfast, and just being us, without a hammer over our heads. Unless there is a hammer, and we just don't know it. Exactly why I call Adam, who doesn't have a wife to stay behind with like Savage, and convince him to join us for the ride.

Ana doesn't ask why.

On some level, I wonder if she isn't relieved, if she doesn't feel what I feel.

When we finally head to the airport, Blake meets us there, and without any prodding on my behalf, he offers Ana a job. "My wife is handling a situation with a client, or she'd be here. We want you to know you have a job if you want it, Ana. And that you have a family here. So go to Denver. Come back if and when you are ready. We'll be here to welcome you."

"Thank you," Ana replies. "And I'll take the job, whatever it is. I'm coming back."

"Done," Blake replies. "You'll like the pay and the people. I promise."

Blake and I share a few words before our little group of four hits the road and do so with mine and Ana's future in our sights.

I should be walking on water and yet, I'm no less unsettled.

Ana, on the other hand, is elated by the job offer, and talking a million miles an hour. Even Kurt seems to approve of the move for her. I think he's happy for Ana. I also think he's leaving again, but at this point, none of us can stop that from happening. Somehow, I think this trip back to Denver is all about a goodbye which is the only reason I didn't push back on it.

Ana doesn't seem to notice I'm unsettled, for good reason.

I've worked hard at ensuring I don't stress her out, for no reason other than I'm selfishly hungry for her laughter and happiness. We're in the air with Kurt and Adam snoozing in the back, when I decide I can't hold back anymore, not when we're about to land back in Denver, where Phillips resides.

I'm about to tell her what's in my head, when she turns to me and says, "It feels like this all ended too easily, doesn't it?"

I glance over at her. "Yeah. Yeah, it does. It doesn't sit quite right."

"I thought maybe it was because I've basically agreed I'm not arresting anyone. I mean my badge says a lot is wrong and I should do something about it. But what? To who? I can't prove much of anything about anyone. Which is always a problem for me. I want to fix what is broken."

"But?"

"I don't know. Maybe that is it, but I'm pretty at ease with walking away from my badge right now.

Surprisingly at ease with it. I feel like I can do more in other places."

"I'd say we land and take off again and lay low a few days," I reply, "but I think Kurt is going to split."

"Of course he is," she says. "I'm not at peace with that, and I'm pretty sure I've buried a ton of baggage over that, we'll deal with later, but it is what it is. We just need to be on alert when we land."

"Agreed. Let's mail your badge back and pay a service to pack you up. We need to get in and get out."

She nods, and for the rest of the flight, our mood is solemn, but expectant and not in a good way.

We land to a dark, snowy night, on a small runway, with an eerie feel to it. I've just powered down the engine when Adam appears. "Houston, we have a problem."

Ana and I share a look that says it all. This is it. This is what we were expecting.

"What does that mean?" I ask.

"Kurt just confessed a problem, the reason he wants to get to The Ranch where he can hunker down and blow up his enemies—his words, not mine. He didn't tell us everything there was to know."

"What the hell, Adam? Spit it out."

"Phillips put a hit out on you and Ana when we left the party. He was done with you. He hired the Invisible Assassin."

That's all I need to hear. I know the Invisible Assassin's reputation. You don't call him, he calls you. Phillips can't just call him and cancel the hit. He has to wait until the Invisible Assassin calls him. We have one of the deadliest assassins on planet Earth hunting us and I logged our fucking flight plan.

**LISA RENEE JONES**

# CHAPTER FORTY-FOUR

## LUKE

Anger surges through me at Kurt's stupidity and arrogance. I surge to my feet with every intention of beating the fuck out of him but Adam's in my path. He puffs up and pushes back. "No, man. That solves nothing. One enemy at a time."

"Starting with him."

"Not now, Luke. I get it. I wanted to do the same thing but first things first. You know he's not our most imminent problem."

Ana catches my hand and her touch reminds me that I can't kill Kurt, but damn it, I want to at least beat the shit out of him. I glance down at her and she says, "Let's just get off this plane, Luke. We're sitting ducks."

I scrub my jaw and step back from Adam. "We could take off again, but the weather is shit and he could just be waiting where we land next."

"Let's get off," Adam votes. "And let's figure out where we're going because it's not The Ranch where they expect us, no matter what Kurt wants. We need to hole up and stand down. I'm going to call Blake and have him find us a spot."

"Yeah," I say. "Call Blake."

He punches in the number and I sit back down to talk to Ana. "This dude is bad. He's never missed a hit. Three days is a long ass time when he's involved. We would have been better off in a safehouse in New York. Kurt drove us right into the palm of his hand."

Adam disconnects. "We're set. I've got the address. Blake already had one of our own picking us up. A guy named Bruno. I've met him. He's an asset. Let's go." He backs out of the doorway and moves into the plane. Ana and I join him outside the door, right along with Kurt.

The minute Ana sees him, she shoves him. "Are you crazy?"

"We need to be on our own territory. He can't touch us out there. I've reinforced everything behind the scenes when you didn't know I was there."

"I didn't know," she says. "That sums up everything wrong with all of this."

I catch Ana's arm and hand her the coat I've retrieved for her. She turns away from Kurt and slides it into place, I don't look at him or I'll hurt him. I bundle up and arm myself and her. Adam opens the door and leans out before updating us on his view.

"Bruno is out there, waiting in our ride. Let's go." He shoves the door all the way open and exits first.

I pull Ana back and force Kurt to exit next. He moves forward and heads outside. Ana is next and I have her rear. The cold is shocking, the wind fierce, the night dark. We're in a line walking toward the SUV when my senses start to buzz. I pull Ana to the left of me, sensing something from the distance, and I don't know what.

Adrenaline surges and it happens. Instinct has me stepping around and in front of Ana right as a bullet hits Kurt. He buckles forward. Adam is closer to the vehicle and he grabs Ana, pulling her with him. I'm aware of her entering the vehicle and all I can think is I can't let Kurt die on her. I throw myself over him, shooting toward the line of trees where this bastard must be hiding. Ana appears again, kneeling next to me, trying to get to Kurt.

"Go back to the truck, Ana!" I shout, but she's not listening.

I have to kill this bastard before he kills her, and that's when I see the tiniest light, a small reflection behind a certain tree. "Cover left!" I shout.

Adam throws himself in front of Ana and Kurt, shooting at the target, while I go right, away from him, where he won't be looking. It works. I blast through the trees and before he knows what's happened, I'm behind him. He turns just as I arrive, almost as if he senses me as I did him, and I put a bullet through his head.

I don't wait to see him fall. Savage isn't with us. We need to get Kurt to a hospital and now, if it's not already too late.

**LISA RENEE JONES**

# CHAPTER FORTY-FIVE

## LUKE

### THREE DAYS LATER...

Kurt lives, but for the rest of my life, I will remember Ana trembling in my arms, as she watched Bruno try to save his life. Turns out Bruno has a good deal of medical training and might be the only reason Kurt survived. Well, David survives. That's the new name Kurt had on his fake ID and the one he chooses to keep.

Today he gets out of the hospital with plans to live in Italy in some spot he bought years before. I'm flying him there, because I'm damn sure not letting him hide out somewhere Ana can't find him. For now, I sit in the hospital room, and watch him act like a cranky old man to the nurse, when she suggests he stay another day. Ana intervenes, a perfect daughter in every way. Kurt knows it. Or he better or I'll still beat his ass for putting us in that situation with the former Invisible Assassin who is now the dead assassin.

I plan to keep him on a leash.

He will not leave Ana again until God takes him.

Or he pisses me off again.

\*\*\*

## ANA

### TWO WEEKS LATER...

I have mixed feelings about the fact that Kurt has been living in a beachfront property in the stunningly beautiful city of Amalfi, Italy while I thought he was dead. But I also have learned a lesson this past year, about letting go of what can do nothing but harm. And after a week of being here, living in the villa off the property—yes, it's a magnificent place—I've come to peace in a way I didn't think possible.

It's on a warm October day—because yes, it actually gets quite balmy in October in Italy—that Luke and I walk the beach. I've officially resigned from the agency and reported what I believe to be criminal activity to the right people who can do something about it through Walker Security. I've been offered pay and a job, that no agent would ever dream of receiving. And I have fallen more in love with Luke than ever before.

With the sand under our toes, we stop to watch the waves crash against the rocks, the crystal blue sea a vicious queen overtaking the shores. It's then that Luke goes down on his knee in front of me. "I know you said yes, but you need another ring."

My heart squeezes and I hold up my finger. "I have the old one, remember? I got it before we left Denver."

"You need a new one that represents the new us. So, Ana, will you marry me?"

I laugh. "Yes, *again,* silly man." He removes the ring on my finger and slides it onto a chain he's pulled from his pocket. He stands and places it around my neck before he produces a ring that is beyond breathtaking. A round center stone that glistens in the sunlight, and must be two carats is surrounded by smaller diamonds.

My hand trembles as he places it on my fingers and then says, "Are you sure you want to marry me?"

"You know I am."

"As in right now?

"Now?" I ask. "What do you mean now?"

He lifts a hand and steps backward and suddenly familiar Walker faces are approaching us, right along with Kurt, and a man holding a bible. Tears find a path down my cheeks and Luke pulls me close. "I'm not letting you get away again, baby."

He has nothing to worry about. On a warm October day in Italy, we stand before friends, who I know are now my family, and we say I do. It is the happiest day of my life. Afterward, we fly to Paris, where our bedroom is glorious enough, that we spend the next twenty-four hours there and never get dressed.

\*\*\*

## ONE MONTH LATER...

The Ranch is up for sale, I've donated a chunk of the money Darius left me, and I've settled into New York living rather well. Luke and I wake on my fifth Sunday morning as his wife, and do what has become our habit. We drink coffee with me in his pajama top and him in his pajama bottom, and watch the news, with every intention of going back to bed, at least for a little while.

That's when the headlines have me turning up the sound, listening to the female newscaster as she says, "In shocking news, the owner of the Denver Lions, Michael Phillips was killed in a car accident today. Details are forthcoming but not yet available.

I turn off the sound. "Luke," I breathe out. "It's just like the way Phillips had people killed. Do you think—"

"Kurt did it? Of course, Kurt did it."

I grab my phone and punch his number. He answers on the first ring. "My little girl. How is New York?"

"Did you do it?"

"If it involved protecting you, the answer is yes. If you want me to apologize, that will never happen. But you can come to Italy to visit and try to convince me otherwise. I think it's a good idea that we don't allow so much time to pass before we see each other again." A woman laughs in the background and he says, "I need to go. Tell Lucifer hello for me. I mean, Luke," he amends as I'm about to object. And then he hangs up.

I glance at Luke. "He did it."

"And so did we, baby." He catches my hand and kisses my ring. "And I think we all made the world a better place, don't you?"

## THE END

\*\*\*

## CHECK OUT MY NEXT RELEASE: THE TYLER & BELLA DUET!

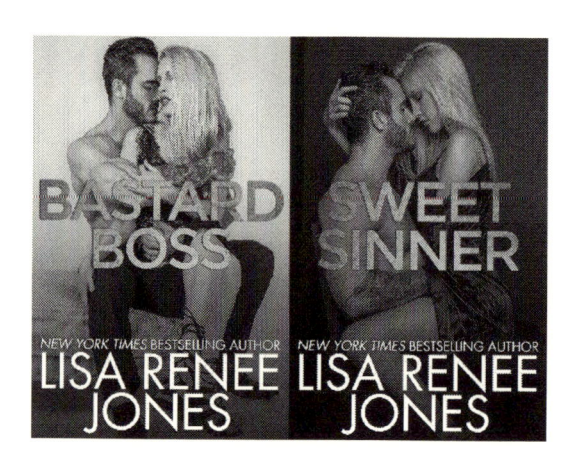

Tyler Hawk is a man with secrets and a dark past. A man who has known tragedy and betrayal. He wants for little, but what he wants is more power, a legacy that is his own, and not his father's. There are obstacles in his way, one of which is the scandal his father left behind and a will with certain demands.

Behind the scenes he is a man on edge, and only one woman sees the truth hidden beneath his strong will and dominant rule. Bella is somehow demanding and submissive, fiery and yet sweet. She can give him everything he wants, she just doesn't know it, not yet, but she will. If she'll just say yes and sign on the dotted line.

PRE-ORDER THE DUET HERE:
https://www.lisareneejones.com/tyler--bella-duet.html

***

AND DON'T MISS THE NEXT BOOK IN THE LILAH LOVE SERIES—THE PARTY IS OVER (BUT NOT THE SERIES)!!

Sometimes a girl just has to get stabby...
Lilah has sworn she's done with that side of her personality.
Then again, maybe not.

FIND OUT MORE HERE: https://www.lisareneejonesthrillers.com/the-lilah-love-series.html#ThePartyIsOver

\*\*\*


Don't forget, if you want to be the first to know about upcoming books, giveaways, sales, and any other exciting news I have to share please be sure you're signed up for my newsletter! As an added bonus everyone receives a free eBook when they sign-up! http://lisareneejones.com/newsletter-sign-up/

# BE THE FIRST TO KNOW!

THE BEST WAY TO BE INFORMED OF ALL UPCOMING BOOKS, SALES, GIVEAWAYS, AND TO GET A FREE EBOOK, BE SURE YOU'RE SIGNED UP FOR MY NEWSLETTER LIST!

SIGN-UP HERE:
http://lisareneejones.com/newsletter-sign-up/

ANOTHER SUREFIRE WAY TO BE IN THE KNOW IS TO FOLLOW ME ON SOCIAL MEDIA:

Facebook: https://www.facebook.com/AuthorLisaReneeJones/
Facebook Group: https://www.facebook.com/groups/LRJbooks
Instagram: https://www.instagram.com/lisareneejones/
TikTok: https://www.tiktok.com/@lisareneejonesbooks
Twitter: http://www.twitter.com/LisaReneeJones
BookBub: https://www.bookbub.com/authors/lisa-renee-jones

# THE NECKLACE TRILOGY

A necklace delivered to the wrong Allison: me. I'm the wrong Allison.

That misplaced gift places a man in my path. A man who instantly consumes me and leads me down a path of dark secrets and intense passion.

Dash Black is a famous, bestselling author, but also a man born into wealth and power. He owns everything around him, every room he enters. He owns me the moment I meet him. He seduces me oh so easily and reveals another side of myself I dared not expose. Until him. Until this intense, wonderful, tormented man shows me another way to live and love. I melt when he kisses me. I shiver when he touches me. And I like when he's in control, especially when I thought I'd never allow anyone that much power over me ever again.

We are two broken people who are somehow whole when we are together, but those secrets—his, and yes, I have mine as well—threaten to shatter all that is right and make it wrong.

FIND OUT MORE ABOUT THE NECKLACE TRILOGY HERE:
https://www.lisareneejones.com/necklace-trilogy.html

# ALSO BY LISA RENEE JONES

## THE INSIDE OUT SERIES

*If I Were You*
*Being Me*
*Revealing Us*
*His Secrets\**
*Rebecca's Lost Journals*
*The Master Undone\**
*My Hunger\**
*No In Between*
*My Control\**
*I Belong to You*
*All of Me\**

## THE SECRET LIFE OF AMY BENSEN

*Escaping Reality*
*Infinite Possibilities*
*Forsaken*
*Unbroken\**

## CARELESS WHISPERS

*Denial*
*Demand*
*Surrender*

## WHITE LIES

*Provocative*
*Shameless*

## TALL, DARK & DEADLY / WALKER SECURITY

*Hot Secrets*
*Dangerous Secrets*
*Beneath the Secrets*
*Deep Under*
*Pulled Under*
*Falling Under*
*Savage Hunger*
*Savage Burn*
*Savage Love*
*Savage Ending*
*When He's Dirty*
*When He's Bad*
*When He's Wild*

## LILAH LOVE

*Murder Notes*
*Murder Girl*
*Love Me Dead*
*Love Kills*
*Bloody Vows*
*Bloody Love*
*Happy Death Day*
*The Party's Over*

## DIRTY RICH

*Dirty Rich One Night Stand*
*Dirty Rich Cinderella Story*
*Dirty Rich Obsession*
*Dirty Rich Betrayal*
*Dirty Rich Cinderella Story: Ever After*
*Dirty Rich One Night Stand: Two Years Later*
*Dirty Rich Obsession: All Mine*
*Dirty Rich Secrets*
*Dirty Rich Betrayal: Love Me Forever*

## THE FILTHY TRILOGY

*The Bastard*
*The Princess*
*The Empire*

## THE NAKED TRILOGY

*One Man*
*One Woman*
*Two Together*

## THE BRILLIANCE TRILOGY

*A Reckless Note*
*A Wicked Song*
*A Sinful Encore*

## NECKLACE TRILOGY

*What If I Never*

*Because I Can*
*When I Say Yes*

## LUCIFER'S TRILOGY

*Luke's Sin*
*Luke's Touch*
*Luke's Revenge*

*eBook only

# ABOUT LISA RENEE JONES

*New York Times* and *USA Today* bestselling author Lisa Renee Jones writes dark, edgy fiction including the highly acclaimed *Inside Out* series and the crime thriller *The Poet*. Suzanne Todd (producer of Alice in Wonderland and Bad Moms) on the *Inside Out* series: *Lisa has created a beautiful, complicated, and sensual world that is filled with intrigue and suspense.*

Prior to publishing, Lisa owned a multi-state staffing agency that was recognized many times by The Austin Business Journal and also praised by the Dallas Women's Magazine. In 1998 Lisa was listed as the #7 growing women-owned business in Entrepreneur Magazine. She lives in Colorado with her husband, a cat that talks too much, and a Golden Retriever who is afraid of trash bags.

Made in the USA
Las Vegas, NV
07 October 2022